SMALL SCALE SINNERS

SMALL SCALE SINNERS

Stories

Mahreen Sohail

A PUBLIC SPACE BOOKS

NEW YORK

A Public Space Books
PO Box B
New York, NY 10159

Printed in the United States of America
First edition, 2025

Stories from this collection first appeared, in earlier forms, in the following publications:
"Najwa" in *Pakistani Literature*, a journal of the Pakistan Academy of Letters
"Basic Training" and "The Funeral" in *A Public Space*
"Sisters" in *Galley Beggar Press*
"Hair" in *Granta*
"Our School Year" in *No Tokens*
"The Dog" in *Post Road*
"A List of Places My Mother Was Old" and "The Newlyweds" in *The Kenyon Review*

A Public Space gratefully acknowledges the support of the New York State Council on the Arts and the individuals, foundations, and corporations whose contributions have helped to make this book possible.

Library of Congress Control Number: 2025940825
ISBN: 9798985976915
eISBN: 9798985976977

www.apublicspace.org

98765432

For my mother and best friend
Shahnaz Sohail

Thank you for making my life possible

SMALL SCALE SINNERS

CONTENTS

OUR SCHOOL YEAR

August

Postmen begin delivering the letters to our houses a week into August, two weeks into the rains that drip sticky and countrywide. Our mothers read between the lines ("shalwar kameez mandatory for girls sixth grade & above") to realize that we are finally turning into women. For our part we understand that something major has changed.

As the new school year comes closer, the mothers host meetings in one another's kitchens to assess the suitability and unsuitability of one another's sons. At night they say their prayers, purse their mouths to blow their breath on us. This will protect you, they say. They have new mantras, ones they try to get us to memorize. We listen to all their advice, store it away to help us cope with what we feel is coming.

YOU MUST NOT EAT PEANUTS

LEARN SELF-SUFFICIENCY

DEVELOP TUNNEL VISION

SUGARCANE WILL GIVE YOU MOUTH ULCERS

BLOOD IS THICKER THAN WATER

By the time we start classes again, our love for them is pulsating like the heat of the summer.

September

Imagine our delight when we find out that the twins who live in the school hostel will be in our class this year. We have won the lottery with them. On our first day back, they are already standing at the back of the classroom, behind rows and rows of desks that seem to have grown larger over the break by virtue of being left alone for many months. Our teacher introduces them to us but there is no need. We already know them as our sisters, we want to be their friends. Their hair falls down their backs like dark rivers and their eyes are a golden brown, lighter than all our eyes.

We handle it badly. We suffocate the twins. We offer them our erasers, our pencils, ask them if they would like to play dodgeball with us—play anything with us? But the girls are impenetrable. The sisters have each other and that, infuriatingly, seems to be enough. They refuse our advances like we are an unwanted new leg, one that will be severed soon.

As the month goes on, they take on the translucent quality of girls who live without their parents. Their wrists grow out of the sleeves of their clothes, clean, sharp, without hair.

Every day, after the last bell rings, we watch them walk out of the school building and in the opposite direction of the school gates. They cross the school grounds to the small brown house otherwise known as the school hostel. A woman opens the door for them. The warden is a mustard-colored spinster famous for her eyes—black and shrunken like raisins.

At home time, our mothers are lined up to receive us with open arms and strained, loving eyes. We cannot help thinking of the twins. We feel ill from how much we want to save them.

October

The school grounds are beginning to go orange, yellow, and red, as if the light from the summer sun is hibernating in the roots of trees and leaves. Whenever we break for prayer, our teachers ask us to pray for them as if they are beginning to believe in our growing sway over God. The teachers hate the twins because they never talk in class and when they do, it is only to whisper to each other. The sisters hold their necks like lovely women who have just become aware of the dips under their collarbones. We beg them to be Cinderella in the end of year school play, rehearsals start soon, and yes, both of them will be perfect for the one part because they are almost the same person. They refuse. Instead, they continue coming to class as the personification of the girls we wish we were, untethered and free.

One day in October, the twins arrive at morning assembly with their nails painted bright pink. Their hands look like small, beautiful claws. The head teacher, whose duty it is to watch us as we march out of our classrooms to assemble in the grounds, makes them step out of the line. Then in the bright October light, she says, You are too young for nail polish. The twins look like they have never been young. This is the worst school in the world, one that cannot recognize the women it is making. The teacher makes them beat the drums in assembly as punishment. They have to strap the drums around their bellies and hit them loudly with sticks. We sing the national anthem and they provide the beat. They keep beating even as we march back to our classrooms. After assembly, they are made to go back to the hostel. They come back with clear nails and pink, wet eyes, as if they have simply rubbed the nail polish into another part of their body. We give them water to make them feel better and watch them sip. They are beginning to realize that we may be a good thing in their lives.

Our own mothers are early that day to pick us up. They spot the girls walking to the hostel. Who are they? they ask. The twins, we say, as if they are an institution. We decide to watch the teachers carefully for further and unprovoked signs of bitchery. Because it is obvious that the twins are orphans, we start carrying knives to school—steak knives, fruit knives, and butter knives—wrapping them first of course in toilet paper so they do not rip through our pockets and our backpacks.

November

We begin to live anticlockwise. Because of high demand, our houses run out of gas in the mornings so our parents cook and shower and shave at night. We are cold all the time, but not as cold as the twins, who are still showing up to class without their required gray cardigans. We give them ours, we take turns. One of us shivers for an hour and then another and then another until the last bell rings. It is a small price to pay because the twins have agreed to be Cinderella.

We hold the rehearsals up on the small mound underneath the old oak tree from our mothers' times. There are swings on this mound. They are never used anymore. Cinderella can hold on to them in the midst of the most powerful throes of her sorrow.

The twins are incandescent and spectacular and we are worried about the other classes finding out about them.

During lunch hour, we make a ring around the actors. When the other classes start to come closer, we take out our knives and hold them so the light bounces off the blade and into the eyes of these spies.

We love teaching the twins how to do the kissing scenes. We tell them that they must put their hand over the prince's mouth (a girl—one of us) and then kiss their own hand so as not to accidentally touch the girl's lips and commit a great sin. The twins think this is very funny because they have already got their periods. We do not like being condescended to, but when they laugh we laugh along with them and this is rewarded because they finally invite us back to their hostel after school. We do not know how to control our happiness and vow to buy them their very own cardigans.

We tell our mothers, who are waiting outside the school gates, that we will be five minutes late. Why? they ask. We tell them about the hostel and they become alarmed. They drag us by our arms to our cars and we think about the twins waiting inside the classroom, us never coming like their poor, dead parents. On the drive home, we ask our mothers to buy the twins cardigans and our mothers say, They are turning you. We bite our tongues so as not to give them the satisfaction of asking, Into what?

December

We are all smart girls so we are not worried about the midterm exams. Our class is outperforming all the other seven sections of sixth grade classes at the school and we are in the top 2 percent of the entire country's sixth grade classes. We are the brightest in the country, The cream of the shining crop, says our esteemed principal, beaming, so we see nothing wrong in continuing our rehearsals through December. The twins haven't spoken to us since we left for our homes without visiting their hostel. They are proud—they have spent years in this world without parents. We have to apologize many times. We are all very sorry. When they finally forgive us we promise we will come to the hostel with them during lunch hour and risk getting expelled. Day scholars are not allowed on hostel grounds. They reluctantly agree. We sense this is our last chance. We cannot afford to ruin this.

It is not raining, but there are some clouds as we walk over to the hostel during lunch, looking back often to make sure the teacher on duty is not paying attention to us. The flat, one-story house looks decrepit up close and is far enough away from the main campus building that we no longer have to worry about being seen. We notice that there is a vegetable patch growing near the entrance. Broccoli heads are shyly peeking at us from near the front door. We garden on weekends, the twins tell us, to our delight. They ask us to wait outside the front door and then they go inside. The wind is blowing and those of us who have lent them our cardigans have to stamp our feet into the ground to stay warm. When we breathe, the air mists around us. The twins come back after ten minutes to say the warden has gone out for her weekly meeting with the vice-principal.

We walk down a corridor lined with rooms that face one another until we stop outside a door that has the twins' names etched on a wide blue plaque. We feel like we are going to fly out of our heads. There are no heaters in the room but each of the sisters has a single bed, a desk, and a cupboard. There is a bear on one of their desks whose fat, distended stomach says I Love You. We look away, trying hard not to wonder where the other twin's bear is. The whole place smells like medicine and there is still half an hour of lunch to go. Let's do Cinderella, we suggest in our great pity for them and they agree. We shove their furniture to the corners of their bedroom and begin the play.

They are very bad actors now. Nerves are making them stupid. They forget the names of the stepsisters and do not weep properly when the stepmother slaps them. The look of joy when the fairy godmother shows up is off-center on their faces. They can tell they are losing us so when it is time for the kissing scene, they hold up their best card. Let's kiss properly, they say, chins tremulous and cheeks aglow as if this sacrifice is costing them something we cannot know. They have our attention again. We watch carefully and the prince blushes and titters. What? say the twins, shining around the shambles of their performance, trying to build themselves up again, You've never kissed someone before?

They put their arms around each other and press their lips together. It's like crushed flowers, the smell of the room, sickly and rotting. One of the twins opens her mouth for her sister and we see her tongue, dark and pink like a worm. We have a white-hot feeling at the base of our stomachs. The warden is suddenly in the room. She can scream louder than all our mothers combined and she is drumming their faces and shoulders with her fists—and so we act. Some of us try to hold the others back. Some of us, we remember, think this is a bad idea. When the first of the knives goes into the warden, it is a clean, smooth invasion. We feel the blood and muscle move aside to let the metal enter. She does not fall to the ground immediately, so we have to try again, once or twice.

The twins are still holding each other but now they are crying too. We borrow clothes from their cupboards and put them on. Some of us button up our cardigans to hide the blood. We lock the body in the room and leave with the twins. We have to be a little rough with them because they will not stop crying. We have to, in fact, threaten them. We wash the knives in their attached bathroom and hold them to their throats and say, Just shut up just shut up okay? Then we lead them out of there. They collect themselves when we emerge back out into the cold open air. They have almost stopped shaking by the time we enter the classroom again.

We beg our English teacher for a free period. Please, miss, we say, we are so behind in math! She is our favorite teacher. She senses that something wild is traveling in each of our bodies. She believes that students are under a lot of strain. We agree with her, we have never felt more strained. We tremble until she tells us it will be okay if we go study in the library very quietly.

The body in the house is still a little warm. The warden looks normal except for the gashes in her stomach and her breasts. We cover her up in the twins' bedsheets and then One two three lift. We take her to the back of the house. One of us watches for straying teachers while the rest of us use our hands and rocks to dig out a hole. We put her in it and cover her up and then take a moment to pray for forgiveness, for her soul, for the twins, and, as usual, for good grades in our midterms.

January

Our success in the midterms is going to be celebrated with a party. It will be on a Tuesday, after school but in the big cafeteria down the road where the senior girls have their dinners and lunches.

The vice-principal has already given her permission. Our mothers have spent the last week preparing. They've baked cakes, cut up fruit and arranged them on platters. On the day, we tell our mothers about the twins not having parents and ask them if we can take them from school and then drop them off again later. They say okay, so after class we pack them into a car with us. They sit in the back seat and our mothers fuss over them on the way to the party. The twins have grown thin over the break. They have a pinched, hurt look on their faces, as if they are being made to gnaw on the bones of things. In the car, they edge away from us and sit together like two chess pieces of the same color.

The party room is decorated in pastels. There are purple balloons strung from the ceiling and a banner that says Halfway to Graduation. Last year, we studied the states of matter in science. We know there are four: solid, gas, liquid, and plasma. We are almost at the plasma level of happiness by the time we have eaten. Only the twins are unhappy. They have not done well on the midterms. They stand a little bit away from us and when we ask them if they want to rehearse *Cinderella* they say No, outright. Even our mothers notice how rude that is because they bring it up after we have driven the sisters back to the hostel. The new warden opens the door. The rumor around school is that the old one had a fight on her walk with the vice-principal in December and walked straight out of the school, leaving all her things behind. This new woman is taller than the old one, in fact the top of her head almost touches the top of the doorway.

February

The twins are acting strange. They have not practiced the play with us for weeks and instead stand vigil near the grave at lunchtime. We hear the biology teacher whisper to the chemistry teacher, This is what happens when you don't have parents. Sometimes they sit near it, under a tree, on their haunches, side by side. One day it rains and one of us sees them run out of the hostel in the morning as we are being dropped off to use their shoes to pat at the ground, even it out. They are worried the body will wash out but our mothers say the rains will stop soon. Spring is coming. The ground is easing up beneath us. We give the twins another chance. We ask them if they'd like to play dodgeball. When they refuse, we have no choice. We tighten our fists around their wrists and track them back from the grave over to the mound. The ghost of this woman will drive you mad, we warn them. We divide ourselves into two teams. The twins are on the team that has to dodge the ball. They stand in the middle and we target them with the ball until they begin to move. Finally, they even laugh.

March

We long to speak to men. We ask the twins where they learned to kiss and they are reluctant to answer. The movies, they finally say when we step on their hands during gym class. We want to practice kissing with real men but only know one who is not related to us. He is the music sir. The music sir teaches us piano. Often, when we get to class, he is sitting in front of his computer, tongue out and eyes a little glazed. We begin to look forward to these lessons and notice carefully who he speaks to and who he doesn't speak to.

It is unlucky that the body of the warden is found behind the hostel before the holidays. The garden keeper runs like a flag, flying toward the school building with a look of such terror that we know it can be nothing else. Immediately we see swarms emerge from the administrative offices. Even Madam Samina, who is teaching us, looks out the window every few minutes, eyes squinting against the great, green expanse of the school grounds.

We have to be alone in rooms with policemen who are kind to us. They ask us questions and call the warden Ma'am Warden. Did you know her? they ask. Yes, we say, though only from afar. Doctors pat us down with thin, cold fingers and put their stethoscopes on our skin. They ask us if we had been hurt by the warden, by any of our teachers. Our mothers cry and cry and cry at home and into one another's arms at the school gates. They ask us over and over again if something has happened to us at school.

The twins disappear the day before the body is discovered. They don't come to class all day and we hear the teachers whispering about their suspicious absence. All of their clothes are still back in the room. The other girls who live in the hostel say they have been murdered. We picture the teddy bear holding its red heart on that desk. We picture someone giving the bear to one or the other of the twins and saying the words *I Love You* while the other one stands there envious and hungry for attention. Maybe they killed each other, we say to the other girls.

We remember how they looked in the room that day, blazing and immodest, two Cinderellas launching themselves at the spinster. We recount the story for the media, the police, the coroner who asks us to retell the stabbing part of it. Why didn't you say anything? everyone asks. We didn't want to get in trouble. We talk about our passion for education and other human interest things like how one of our main worries at the time of the incident was making sure we could do the hardest yoga poses in PE. We cry inside television screens around the country. What poor girls, everyone repeats, until we begin to believe in our martyrdom.

April

The news of the murder seeps into every corner of the school. This is the final story: Before they left, the twins dug up the body and carried it to the front of the house to lay it near where the broccoli had grown the winter before. Now the patch is overrun with tomatoes, their red and green a backdrop to the newscasts that are still appearing nightly. We believe that the twins killed the warden. Even the teachers admit it. They keep breaking off in the middle of lessons to say, There was something strange about those girls. They need something concrete to pin the crime on them, so we tell them about the kissing. This confirms it. It was the devil, our mothers agree, and they slap us when we get home. How could you watch that? they ask. The discomfort of that moment in their room comes back to us in sharp clarity and we push it back down.

The authorities have been taking chalk from our classrooms to draw an outline around the hostel every morning since the body was discovered so the crime scene stays fresh. The other hostelites watch from their windows with grim, lost faces. It is unanimously agreed upon that the twins were prophets, or witches. Something transient. They probably knew the murder was going to happen and still did not stop it. At night, each of us lies alone in our bedroom and thinks about how they put us in that room and then made us hot and angry with desire.

May

That cold gray evening is far away now, as if someone has lobbed it across time. We were not holding the knife. The twins began to kiss and we felt ashamed. We had been taught the wrongness of this so we pulled them apart but they began to fight and twist in our arms, as if possessed. When the warden walked in, they stabbed her and said, You are not our mother. Their voices became deep and harsh. The woman wept as she died. She said, Please. No. Don't. Each word a sentence. She looked exactly like our mothers. We said, Stop, please! but the bitches just kept going. This is what happens to girls who live in hostels.

We weren't allowed to go near the chalk outline. Anyway the area had been surrounded by reporters and cameramen and policemen for two months. There are many policemen. At first, there are twenty, standing in a line and bending to the ground to touch the grass, a small army of men with worry in their faces and guns leaning across the lengths of their bodies. Slowly, the men begin to disperse. If at first there were twenty, after two weeks there are ten, then after a month and a half there are only two—small, ready sentries visible from a distance because of the smoke they inhale from cigarettes and then expel from their mouths into the warm air.

The two policemen sit there with their feet over the shallow hole in the ground. They stand when they see us coming and straighten their faces. We leave immediately, afraid they will tell our teachers, but we go back again after another week has passed.

This time the men aren't there. Perhaps they are on their lunch break, perhaps they have left. The yellow tape roped around the grave has ripped in one part and is swinging in the wind like an extra loose gate. The hole is dry and filled with decaying leaves.

June

The production of *Cinderella* is a big success. The prince, the fairy godmother, the ugly stepsisters, and the stepmother speak to an empty spot in the room and it is enchanting. Even we are moved. The whole school gives us a standing ovation. This will be the summer of our becoming. We cry afterward like the good girls that we are.

THE DOG

We decided to use the word *indisposed* when people called to ask about our father. We had a meeting in the kitchen, my brother and I, during which we both agreed the word sounded gentle and worldly. At first they called as usual, of course. They wanted to know the date and time of a conference, ask him about some matter of business, just chat. To those ones, we said, Sorry, he's in the toilet. When they called again, we said, He is feeling sick. The third time we upped the ante: Indisposed.

Then, there was the dog. We'd bought him to be a guard dog, but he mostly stayed in the empty plot of land next to our house and now that our father was suffering from compromised immunity, we could not go near him without taking extreme measures. For example, I had to shower immediately after petting him. This was a hassle. My brother never went near him anymore, and my father yelled at the animal from afar. We decided the only thing to do was to post a notice at the vet's: Labrador, one year old, untrained. Free. No one called until a week had passed. My brother answered the phone. His face became sour when whoever was on the other end started to speak. Lately he'd become irritable. In fact, he had been the greater advocate of the word *indisposed.*

Give them as little as possible and then take it away, he'd said. During our meeting in the kitchen, I asked him, Don't you want to be like our father? This was a double-edged sword, I could tell by his face: Would you rather be wonderful and soon to be dead or less wonderful but always alive?

It's about the dog, he said as he handed the phone to me. I didn't want to be the sort of person who lost interest in things. I had brought the dog home with love and the best of intentions but as my father's illness progressed, it had become easier and easier to see the poor animal dirty and unhappy. I was polite to the lady on the phone, and honest. I told her my father was sick, and I did not feel the lump in my throat I normally felt when I said those words. It was cold inside the house, though the smell from the gas heater had already spread through the rooms. Someday I was going to leave this country and this city and this house, and my brother was going to marry the girl he had been in love with for ten years. I did not, of course, tell the woman these particular things, but I repeated that the dog was free. From the other room, my dad cackled. Free in theory, he said through big breaths. I told her she would have to love it and care for it. I knew these were things people looking to adopt dogs wanted to hear. On the phone, the woman sounded cultured. She spoke English with hardly an accent and mentioned the local vet as if he were an old friend. Finally she asked, When can I come see him? I told her we were always at home but also added that she would have to wear a mask when she came inside because of my father. Of course, she said.

Well? asked my brother. He was sitting by my father's bed, and they were playing Ludo. My father's green figures moved closer and closer to home, and my brother kept his eyes on the board even as he spoke to me to make sure my father didn't nudge them out of turn. We were unflappable as a family. We approached everything face up, like fish on hooks angling toward the sun. She said she'll be here in a few hours. My father coughed. Thank God that animal won't haunt us anymore. Yeah, said my brother. Just give it to her quick and let her go. Don't let her play with the dog for too long or she may not want him.

The truth was the dog was wild. We hadn't had the patience or energy to train him so he jumped on whomever he saw and had once made my back bleed by grazing his nails on my spine. We would have to put him on a leash and make sure he didn't get too close to the woman. And tell her she can't bring it back, said my brother, keeping his eyes on the dice. I nodded.

The doorbell rang at 6:00 p.m. I had cleaned the house a little for her arrival but I was still aware that it smelled like a hospital, possibly even bile. At the door, I handed her the mask ceremoniously and readjusted mine. My brother and I usually walked around with our surgical masks only hanging off one ear, the ends of them flapping near our chins and necks. The dog is outside, I said, but won't you come in? She was shorter than I and was wearing a black coat, expensive, the kind you buy from abroad. She wasn't wearing gloves, and there was a ring on her finger, chunky and too trendy for a woman her age. I felt immediately self-conscious, though of course we were not wanting for money. We were simply down on our luck. How many times had my father said No health, no wealth when we were growing up?

She stepped into the house without a pause and this took me off guard. My brother was just coming out of the kitchen, popping open a can of Coke. Our father was rattling around in his sleep in the next room. I'm so sorry about your father, she said. She spoke to me as if I were young and I heard my brother stop in the doorway, too. We were young, we were young. This phrase circled around in my head. The past year had been full of ugly words I tried to keep at a distance. I only cried on the way to and from work, and even then, I thought, it probably didn't count because no one could see me.

Can I meet him? She looked at me, glancing once at my brother. It took me a second to realize she meant my father.

At this my brother came forward. He's dying, he said, abruptly. What do you mean, can you meet him? But she seemed so soft spoken, I wondered, why not? I turned to my brother. Why not? My father hadn't met anyone in many months. It would be nice for him to see this woman, a woman his own age. Maybe he would feel passion. She was good looking with a short dark bob cut that reached the ends of her ears.

My brother's face changed into something I couldn't recognize, and outside, the dog barked once. I led the stranger into my father's room. At first, when my father became sick, we had talked obsessively about the illness. We loved the word *manage*; it contained all the multitudes that escaped us. But soon, we became tired and our mouths drooped. We talked instead about Ludo and the day-to-day business of keeping the plants around the house alive, the lack of gas, what was to be done about the shelves in the attic. This woman could be a miracle. She was warm and from outside, where people told one another what they wanted as if these were achievable things. Recently a friend of mine had called and said she wanted to have a one-night stand with a man she had been working with for ten days. Why isn't it possible, she asked, for women to have that in this country? Exactly, I said. We talked about it for an hour and then I felt lighter. It was nice to believe scandal could hold the longest and fiercest sway in the world.

When the woman walked into my father's bedroom, my father was asleep but the curtains were not drawn. My brother stayed, Coke can in hand, standing now by the doorway of the kitchen staring into the room. The woman was not at all fearful or tentative, instead she seemed very sure of herself, as if she had a job to do and she knew how to do it. I was relieved she was in the house and felt a little sad that she would soon leave with the dog. She adjusted the mask on her face and went straight to the bed. Hello, sir. My father opened his eyes and blinked once or twice. She touched my father's shoulder and sat on the edge of the bed. I'm sorry you're ill.

Thank you. He blinked again. He did not know who she was or why she was there, but she saved him from the embarrassment of pretending to know. Yes, I'm here for the dog. You must be very sad to be giving him away. At this he laughed. I'm sad all the time. Do you think a dog makes much difference? I thought, How many people talk about sadness as a daily habit? I'm sorry, she said. It must feel terrible to be dying. I was surprised to hear my own anger in the room: He's not dying. The woman looked at me, eyes large over the blue of the mask. Oh, she said, I'm sorry.

I wanted to slap her then. He's not dying, my brother repeated, although he had said the exact opposite a few minutes ago. He came and stood next to me and we faced her together, and from the bed I saw my father close his eyes again, a small smile on his face. He always said we were going to save him. Please, I said, let me take you to the dog. My tone was final and the woman got up, just a busybody after all, here for the show. She stood slowly. She did not seem like she was ever asked to leave houses, even politely. Yes, she said, hand pressed to the mask. She turned to my father. I hope you get better. He nodded. Thank you. My brother squeezed my hand. Our lives were like clocks and we were waiting and waiting for someone to put the battery in so we could look at the time again.

I led her outside into the cold air. The dog jumped up and down at the woman with its muddy paws. At first, the woman was shocked but she managed it quite well. She made small clucking noises with her mouth and ushered the dog into the back seat of her car. He was a shade of copper now, probably from a combination of rain and mud. I did not feel anything as she put the car in reverse, first carefully taking off the mask and putting it next to her on the passenger seat. Good luck, she said, cheerily waving a small hand at me. Bye, I said. The dog sat quietly in the back seat, tongue hanging out. I imagined the air in there becoming hot and tangy from his breath. After her headlights disappeared, I didn't stand out there for too long before going back inside. The lights were all on in the room and my father was wide awake. The two of them were playing Ludo again. There was another life out there. I could feel it sometimes, right before I went to bed: almost tangible but just out of reach. In this other life he was also old and sitting up in bed on a Tuesday night, my brother across from him, both of them laughing but neither of them aware that one would soon die. Religion, I had wanted to say to the woman when she came in like a prophet, has no place in this house. Here, we were simply living many lives, side by side. In one life, he was this amount of sick exactly. In the other, less so, and in the third, he was absolutely fine. In some lives, our mother was still alive, too, and we lived in a smaller, more compact house with central heating. The dog was well trained and sat when told to sit and fetched bottles of water from the fridge. With so many lives happening all the time around us, how dare I be ungrateful? This was the key, I thought as I joined them at the Ludo board, picked up the small yellow figures and placed them, exactly four, on my side. The key was to rest in the space between lives for a little while, and then maybe you would eventually be able to go on.

HAIR

The boy's mother is sick and has lost all her hair. In solidarity, he decides to cut his off too. He thinks this is the least a son can do for a sick mother. The first person he tells is his girlfriend of one year. I'm going to donate my hair to my mother, he says, and is worried to see tears rise in her eyes. She had told him soon after they met that the first thing she liked about him was his shoulder-length hair, how it lay wild and free on his head, caused people on the street to glance back at them when they walked together. The boy worries that she is actually horrified at the idea of him cutting off his hair. But it's my mother, he thinks, it's my choice. Before he can make a case, the girl, a nice girl from a middle-class family who knows how to drop meaningful hints coyly (my parents are looking for a boy for me), finally says, I think cutting your hair for aunty would be a wonderful thing to do.

The mother is in bed with the smooth baldness of her newly shaved scalp, a scarf loosely draped across her neck. She does not know her son has gone to donate his hair and is not the sort of mother who would approve. She does not believe one person being ill is a reason for another to act ill. And anyway, if she did know, she would have enough faith in the girl to stop her son. She likes the girl. She thinks maybe in a few years they will marry, but the mother does not know if she will be alive for the wedding. A pure-cut line of steel runs through the mother and she knows the world moves on and on, so there is no need for theatrics, no need really for anything while she is so tired, staring up at the ceiling for hours on end. Odd now to think that when her husband built the house, she found the textured cream paint a little creepy, even said so to him then, The texture is a little creepy, a statement that the husband, in his usual overbearing style, overrode. But now she understands why he chose the paint, maybe. It's easy for her to fall asleep while trying to follow the pattern it makes on the ceiling.

The salon is unisex. The boy and girl unclasp their hands when they enter and the boy explains at the counter what he wants. He says, I want to make sure my hair can be donated. His hair is tied up in the usual bun and he loosens it when he talks so the curls fall to his shoulders. I want it to be a wig for my mother. The woman behind the counter calls her associate's name and they descend on the boy and touch his head gently, with some sadness, as if he is their pet and they are about to say goodbye. Behind them, the girl stands with her own long, straight hair shining down her back, almost down to her knees. She rubs her arms as if she is cold. She feels herself rising to the middle of this story and floating in the very center of it.

The husband watches the wife sleep. The house is nicest when she is asleep because he worries less about her and knows for a fact that she is resting, and for a little while at least he manages to forget that she is dying. This is also more bearable than watching her lie awake and worry about dying. The husband is unsure if he has loved anyone in his life, at least in the way he thought he would love when he was younger, but now he thinks that maybe this is what love is supposed to be; you build a life around a person and when they threaten to go, you panic that you will become untethered and they will take you with them. If this is it, then he would prefer to go back to being a stranger to his wife.

The hairdresser winds his fingers through the boy's hair. He stretches out the curls, wets them with a spray bottle, and combs through the hair with his fingers again. The boy looks at the man's face. Will it be possible? he asks. The man tries hard to look matter-of-fact. I'm sorry, he says, your hair has to be at least twelve inches long when the length is taken from the nape of your neck.

The girl feels her heart squeeze. The thing is—the thing is, she knows already that she wants to be with the boy, and while mostly her heart is compassionate for his family, some part of her is also thinking, This is my time. The boy is nineteen years old this year. She is eighteen, and most of her friends are dating the men they believe they will marry. Surely a man she is here for right now in the most impossible moment of his life will want her by his side forever, the girl thinks. She rearranges her face so that it resembles scissors, like something about to cut herself or the boy, and says, I'll do it. The boy looks at the girl's hair and says, You don't have to do this, but it is weak. They switch chairs and the hairdresser is swishing the towel around the girl's neck and spraying her hair with water and tying it in a ponytail at the nape of her neck.

Are you ready? he asks and she nods. Then he cuts it all off in two quick strokes. She closes her eyes for a second, but really she feels like a saint. She feels quite amazing, as if she has finally transcended petty relationships and is now in the midst of the truest, greatest love she is capable of.

The watching boy realizes he has made a big mistake. She looks terrible.

The wife does not open her eyes even though she feels she must get up soon to cook. She drifts in and out of consciousness, but even so it is easy to imagine that she will be better after this day passes. Maybe even in a few moments. I would love daal chawal, she says sleepily, actually wanting to get up and make it herself, but her husband, sitting by her side, stands quickly. If you'll just go back to sleep, he pleads, I'll make it for you. He heads to the kitchen and pulls down the lentils from the top cupboard, pulls out the rice and looks at the two items for a moment. He wishes for a second that his son were home. It would be so lovely to have him here, both of them healthy and men, which sometimes feels like the natural order of things or, if not the natural order of things, at least some order of things.

The girl feels freer with short hair. The hairdresser has not let the cut hair fall to the ground. He is still holding it in his fist so it descends like a black ribbon. It can't touch the floor, he says, that's a no-no for wigs. We'll send it away and they'll mail you the wig in a week. The girl looks in the mirror at the boy's face and he seems ashen, wrecked, and the girl feels triumphant. This is it, she thinks, what a small sacrifice for him to love me! The girl bargains in her head all the time about the boy—if I do this he will do that, and if I do that he will do this—so sometimes it can feel like he is lodged like a small, sharp rock in her head. The haircut has made his presence lighter, as if a little bit of him has also been cut away with her hair.

The hairdresser puts the hair on a shelf, labels it with the boy's mother's name, and he comes back to the girl. Her hair looks uneven. Would you like a bob cut? he asks and she says, Sure. She decides to try something fun. She gets an asymmetrical bob with the longer side touching her chin and the other side riding up to her ear. She does look a little experimental, like someone who could break up with the boy, a person who could live alone for a few years. The hairdresser asks if he can take a picture of her and she says Yes, so he takes the towel off and swivels her around and takes out his phone. You'll find this online by this evening, he says and the girl beams. The girl and the boy hold hands on their way out of the salon, their path lit up by the smiles of the salon staff.

The boy's hand feels like it is crawling with ants. He remembers how the night before, he had kissed the girl on her stomach and her back had arched a little off the bed and when it did her hair had lain thick under her, half on the mattress and half stuck to her spine, where he had brushed it off carelessly. The thing is the boy knows it is a terrible thing to like people based on their looks, and she is an amazing person. Which is worse, he wonders, to like someone less because they are ugly or because they have become better than you during what is supposed to be the most character-building, mother-losing year of your life?

He decides while they drive home and as he takes sidelong glances at her, that he could like it more if it was symmetrical. As if on cue she asks, Do you think it's too experimental?

———

The mother wakes and through a haze she can see her son and her husband and the girl standing there. The girl looks younger somehow. The husband is holding a plate of food and the smell of the food makes the mother sick. She turns on her side and vomits. I don't think your mother likes my hair, the girl says.

It looks great, the boy's father tells the girl, still holding the plate. Yes, the boy lies, it does. All three of them reach for the wastepaper basket filled with vomit but none of them actually touch it. The mother pants, spent, on the bed.

That night the boy drives the girl back to her house. The maid opens the main door and avoids looking at the boy. The house staff is supposed to pretend the girl is pure and does not do anything with the boy except go out to public places and eat. The girl's parents pretend this too, or at least the mother does, and later she tells the girl's father, She will never get married if we keep her locked up in the house. Things have changed, and our daughter knows her limits.

The boy says hello to the girl's mother, who is standing near the kitchen, and the mother says hello as usual, but then her gaze falls on her daughter and she lets out a small scream. What did you do? The girl hesitates, then speaks quickly, shyly. His mother needed a wig. And the mother, who is smart, tries to redo her reaction so that she seems proud to have a daughter who can make this sort of sacrifice, but really, the mother also feels immeasurably sad. All that long, beautiful hair.

The girl's hair is sent to a wigmaker in the middle of the city who threads each strand so it bands together again, cohered into a new shape for the recipient. The wigmaker reads the file of the recipient of the wig: 62; housewife. Sixty-two-year-olds like layers in their hair, he thinks, so he cuts in a few layers and then gently puts the wig in crepe paper, lays it down in a wooden box filled with small spheres of Styrofoam. He tapes the box shut and presses on the address label.

The next day the boy kisses the girl on the lips when she is visiting his house. How's your mother? she asks when they are alone in his room and he says, Good, and then he kisses her again. When he puts his face near the side of the bob that is shorter, he feels as if he is going out with a person without a limb.

I love this, he says and keeps kissing her, and she leans up and kisses him back. His parents are in the other room so she bites his shoulder to keep from crying out during sex. Later, when she sleeps, her shoulders and neck remain damp. He quietly gets out of bed and he takes scissors from his drawer. She is turned onto the side of her face with the shorter hair length. He lifts the longer hair off her face and cuts it, taking care to hold the cut strands so they don't fall back on her face and wake her. The moment he cuts her hair he feels the deep satisfaction that only comes from having made something even again. She does look slightly better, though he's done a messy job. This is fine, he thinks, it will grow back. He throws the hair he has cut into the bin.

After throwing out the hair, the boy goes to his parents' room. The two of them are playing cards, though the mother has to be prompted to make a move by the father. Your turn, the father says every few minutes and the mother stares at him blankly before saying, Oh yes, and concentrating hard on the hand that she has been dealt. Okay, the boy thinks, sitting on the bed with his parents, they're fine.

How is the girl? the father asks and the boy says, Good, good, good, three times in quick succession. He leaves to go back and watch the girl sleep.

Is this how sociopaths behave? He thinks about this while she is asleep and wonders if he could kill her if he had to and he thinks the answer is no, though you never know how you will react to things. This is the first girl he has ever slept with and he has cut her hair without permission. Who knows what else is inside him: a person who beats up women, a person who actually wants his mother to die now, a person who often wakes up thinking enough is enough.

The girl wakes and flies at him: Are you insane? And the father comes running: Why are you disturbing your moth—, but he doesn't have time to finish his sentence because he is struck by his son's girlfriend's crying face and the fact that one side of her head looks as if someone has shorn a plant with little care. She looks like a small child who has been deliberately wounded. Suddenly, the father remembers again that he wanted to marry someone else when he was younger, a woman who lived nearby, but his own mother at the time had said no, presenting instead this wife whom he does love now and the father thinks that maybe this is what happens, we run circles around one another as a family, young old young, and here is his son in the middle of losing someone like he was once in the middle of losing someone and how they are both losing the mother, young old young.

From the other room the mother calls and the girl leaves, still wailing. Without a word to each other the father and son present themselves to the dying woman and say, Everything is fine, you should go back to sleep.

The girl goes back home and falls into the arms of her mother, who says, What happened? but not before running her hand over the girl's head. This is the thing, the mother says, you gave him too much power, and the girl says, What power? And the mother knows that the daughter will have to cobble together a personality of dynamite one day to get through life successfully—remember if Muhammad cannot go to the mountain the mountain will come to Muhammad, the winner is always a man named Muhammad—but her poor baby, My poor baby, she says. She cradles her daughter's head in her lap and says softly, It will grow back, as if hearts are things that grow back and men are roots you can pull out of the ground and toss away.

The wig arrives at the house on a day when the father and the son are home and the mother is feeling better. The father brings in the box and puts it on the bed and carefully cuts the tape on the carton with a little razor blade, sets that aside and opens the box, pushes aside the crepe paper. He moves the box onto the mother's lap. With a cry of delight the mother lifts the wig with her bruised hands. It's beautiful, she says, patting the hair, oh, it really is beautiful. She begins to cry and tells the boy, You must call her and tell her she is beautiful. She takes off her scarf and fixes the wig on her head and by the doorway, her son leans against the door. For a second the only thing the room consists of is how happy his mother is.

When they bury her, they bury her with the wig. The girl does not come to the funeral.

The boy even calls the girl and tells her about the funeral before it happens, but she hems and haws, having discovered some hardness in the story, some new asphalt to coast on. She is learning that she does not want to settle into adulthood with nothing to show for her youth except some pictures of herself in varying poses with hair at different lengths. Here it is long, here it is short, here it is gone, and now it's back again. She is learning not to be kind for the sake of being kind and her mother is sad about this hardness that has arisen in her daughter, but you cannot unlearn a lesson, and her daughter is already practicing how to wield this lesson in the world.

The boy breathes a sigh of relief immediately after the funeral and wonders about all the paths to tragedy. For example, the hair was dead when it became a wig and for a while, in between, when she got better for a week, his mother used to hang it up on the coatrack carefully at night and he would imagine that because it was dead it would soon begin to fall, strand by strand, onto the floor.

By now, the boy thinks, after a month has passed, it must be caked in mud so many feet deep in the ground, damp and splitting.

Or maybe if he and his father dug up the grave in a year's time there would be nothing there at all except the hair once given from a woman to a woman, still long, shining and straight, also some bones.

The girl's hair grows. She massages coconut oil into it nightly, sometimes uses yogurt and fenugreek. It grows down her back, and for her wedding three years later she has it up in a princess braid, pinned a thousand different ways so her husband has to spend the first two hours of their wedding night helping her take it out. It crackles, hard with hair spray, underneath her when they lie in bed together, too tired to touch. When they divorce three years later, she cuts it off, so it looks like a boy's, dyes it bright red so people say, This is what happens, in whispers behind her back. She travels soon after, the dye fading now in the short stumpy hair, feeling invisible and light.

The hair is just touching her shoulders when she meets someone again. It grows faster than it has ever grown when she is in love and happy, when she is pregnant with her first daughter.

The girl and her husband shave their daughter's head four days after the birth. Her husband holds the baby's head as if it is a bird, the blade sharp and keen across the soft malleable temple.

When the girl breastfeeds her daughter, her hair begins to turn white, as if the baby is leeching the color out, and soon it is falling in thick clumps and sticking to the shower drain. Pregnancy hair is short-lived, a friend—a mother three times over by then—tells her on the phone. The girl cuts it off again. Then it grows slowly. She lets it wisp onward for years, through new jobs, illnesses, nights spent lying awake, her mother's death, and then begins to dye it black. She asks her daughter if she looks like Madonna, young old young, and the daughter (now a teen) says, Who is Madonna?

When the girl dies, it is this daughter who bathes her, who curls shampoo into the soft wrinkles set deep in her mother's still scalp. Hope is always a daughter with an unbroken heart. In the distance the line of mountains snakes on across the horizon and reaches, singing, for the women too.

SISTERS

Sadia as Impending Disaster: Something falls from the top shelf of a military ammunition facility in Rawalpindi and hits a grenade, which hits something else, which sets off missile after missile, and my sister, Sadia, is launched into the world.

Sadia as Newborn: Sadia is born the exact moment Ojhri Camp explodes. My mother thinks the bang is coming from inside herself, that she has killed her firstborn, or her firstborn is killing her. Her ears ring. The attendant nurse calls for Allah, her eyes wild. Outside, in the waiting room, my father paces in circles, going, Ya Allah Reham.

Sadia as Afterbirth: I am born two years later. My parents bring me home to Sadia. The country has already sewn itself back up at the seams after the accident with the missiles.

Sadia as Playmate: When she is seven and I am five, Sadia makes me clean the house when our mother isn't home. She is not religious but she has strong leadership tendencies. Clean girls are good girls, she says, hovering over me with a broom.

Sadia as Adolescent: At thirteen, Sadia comes into our room holding up her underwear, white cotton with a bright red spot on it. She waves it around like a flag and her surrendering words are, I am dying. No one has ever spoken to us about periods. I burst into tears. Sadia seems beatific, a true martyr, my leader in life. In the midst of my tears I remember that if she dies I won't have to share the room. Our mother walks in looking for a comb, spots Sadia waving around the bloody underwear. And when our mother's expression changes to one of—what? fear?—we both know it to be true: Sadia *is* dying. The room, I think, this room is so big and soon it will all be mine!

Sadia as Killer: Sadia almost kills a man. We are both outside, I am fourteen and Sadia is sixteen and an uncle walks up to the gate. He is not a real uncle, just a man our father knows who lives in the house three doors down from us. He hangs around the gate and says, What do you girls like to do? Sadia is already too cool for him but I say, Watch movies. The sun beats down on his head and he says, Like blue movies? And from our classmates at school who have nose rings, we know *blue movies* is code for porn, and I am embarrassed and ashamed. But Sadia, quick as a flash, is by the gate and she says, Yes, and then she says, Come closer, and the uncle does. His eyes are so happy, probably the happiest they've ever been. When he's close enough, Sadia leans over, something glints in her hand and it is the Swiss Army knife she got from school for spelling e-x-t-r-a-p-o-l-a-t-e correctly. Through a gap in the gate, she pokes it in the man-uncle's knee. Ow, he says, like a wounded dog, ow. The leg leaks blood. I will have you randis killed, he says while leaving. Sadia looks at me and says, No one should hurt us. We are breathing hard.

Sadia as Replica: It's true what they say. Sisters are cast from the mold their mother shed a long time ago. A study in parts: a lip here, a mouth there, what lovely eyes we have.

Sadia as Marriage Prospect: When she is eighteen, men begin to propose marriage to Sadia as if a target has materialized on her forehead. You will be beautiful too, people tell me consolingly when they sit in our drawing room, eyeing her. One man and his family drape themselves across our sofas. They spin lies out of their mouths, Our son makes twenty-seven lakh a month, he went to UC Berkeley. Sadia nods at the family, says, I got into UC Berkeley too and so I can't get married because I have to study, before getting up and leaving the room. Later our mother slaps both of us when she catches us laughing. When we are finally alone Sadia lies on the bed, the stinging red palm an alarm on her cheek and says, The thing is, I am in love with someone else.

Sadia as Lover: She has seen him on the terrace of his house from the terrace of our house, lifting weights and skipping rope. She takes me upstairs to show him to me in the evening and says, Ah, when he appears. It is clear that he knows she is watching. He jumps against the orange sky, his body thin and wiry under his clothes. He's trying to build muscle, she says and giggles as if she has known him for years. Have you spoken to him? I ask her in my lightest tone. I understand then that she has been initiated into the world of true movie-like love and left me behind. When I look at her, I imagine another version of myself looking at me looking at her and feel sadder than ever.

Sadia as Teacher: She explains the boy to me. When I remind her that she doesn't know him, she says, Can't you tell he is not like that, touching the curve of her neck as if he lives there. She smiles and smiles and smiles. She says, He would come over if I asked him to, even with just my eyes. I stare at him in the evenings with my sister, suspicious and alarmed: What is he trying to build muscles for? What if she marries him and I have to live in this house all alone for many years because no one wants to marry me?

Sadia as Disobedient Daughter: Sadia spends an actual year and a half staring at him. When she is twenty-one, she finally tells our mother: I want to marry him, Ammi. If you don't let me, I will anyway. And our mother bursts into tears and says, The day you were born was a black day for a reason. That night the whole house contracts and mourns, our small family set aflame by love at first sight.

Sadia as Home: Sadia curls into me every night and hugs me around the waist and says, You are my best friend in the whole world. I stay silent, go to sleep with her going, Please be on my side.

Sadia as Obedient Daughter: Sadia stirs sugar into tea for our father, plies him with shami kebabs as if he is a guest in his own house. I know what you're trying to do, he says, but your mother knows best.

Sadia as Adviser: You should study abroad, she tells me, when I am applying to colleges. Go to UC Berkeley. She says this like a defeat, as if she has been forcibly strapped to the line of her sight, which remains on that other terrace. You don't even know if he likes you, I tell her with disgust. *You* go to UC Berkeley.

Sadia in Winter: Sadia eats mandarins in front of the heater and leaves the peels there on the rug so the whole house smells like roasted orange rinds. This is the smell that I think of often, the smell of the year before Sadia gets married, the last real year of my life.

Sadia in Protest: Months pass, and Sadia stops eating. Who is he? my mother says, trying to slap her out of it. Are. You. Fucking. Him. You. Slut. Nobody slaps me or comes near me, but maybe that is because I am the only real daughter now.

Sadia as College Student: I enroll in the same college as Sadia, where she continues to ace all her exams. She's very popular. Sometimes when I walk across the quad, I see her with her friends, up on the grassy area. They are obsessed with practicing running jumps, God knows why. Sadia hikes up her shalwar, her little leg hairs wave in the air, she runs and then leaps across the grass. I can see the other girls' mouths open and close in astonishment. To what end, I wonder, as the classes drone on around us.

Sadia as Idiot: The boy from the terrace comes over! He brings his parents too. The parents smile at the room and extend an offer: We would like to ask for your daughter's hand in marriage. I have to bite my tongue to keep from giving them *my* hand. Maybe that would be funny. The boy is thinner close up, all those years jumping and nothing to show for it. Let us think about it is what our parents say to these other parents. The boy and Sadia smile at each other. No rope in his hands, just my sister's life. Did you see how respectfully the family sat on the sofas? she asks me afterward, spinning round and round in our room.

Sadia as Confidant: I tell Sadia I am in love with the brother of a friend of mine the night after our parents agree to her match with the boy from the rooftop. We are both staring at the ceiling from our respective beds. She laughs. I never forgive her for knowing that I am lying. Not for the rest of my life.

Sadia as Bride: All of Sadia's friends come to the wedding and dance frenetic circles around her shining self. I dance too. Later the couple says yes to each other, and then they sit on the sofa on the stage; the boy a reed, waiting to be picked, my sister next to him, willing and able. I take every chance I get to stuff sweets in her mouth. Even when she says stop, I don't, trying to sugarcoat the fact of her impending departure.

Sadia as Absence (I): That night after I get home from the wedding, I go upstairs and find the surprise she has left for me: there is a new king-size bed in our room, our two twins are nowhere in sight. There is a note on the bed: "Of course, my baby sister gets a dowry too. Love always, Sadia." I fall asleep trying to decide whether the gift is thoughtful or cruel.

Sadia as Absence (II): Sadia comes over with her new husband and they drape themselves across the sofas as guests in our house. She wears gold bangles and carries mithai. When we get a moment alone, just me, her, and our mother, I ask her why she is behaving like an aunty now. She leans in and says, I don't kiss and tell, but boy that first night was good. My mother and her peal into laughter. When the couple leaves, I watch her tuck her arm into the bow of his elbow. I realize then that all this time I have been watching her, and she hasn't spared a thought for me at all.

Sadia as Absence (III): At night I dream of Sadia jumping off a terrace. She takes the leap while calling my name and I struggle in my bed to wake up.

Sadia as Soother: She says, It's 3:00 a.m. Of course I'm alive. Is everything okay? The panic in her voice is soothing. I manage to go back to sleep.

Sadia as Wife: Sadia and my mother talk on the phone. She asks my mother about doctors, about recipes, about how to starch clothes properly. When she comes over to take us shopping in her new family's car with her new family's driver, I notice her purse is missing the Pakistan Is My Mother badge that's always been pinned to it. What happened to it? I ask, and she shrugs. Grow up, she says. And then later, by way of apology, How is the last year of college going?

Sadia as Pregnant Woman: The doctor says Sadia has to take calcium and folic acid because the baby is leeching calcium out of her to grow stronger. She is twenty-four and I am twenty-two. It's true, there are holes in her teeth, her knees crack when she gets up. For the first time, I feel sorry for her. She can sense it. She becomes quiet around me. Once, she is over and fanning herself in the June heat, her stomach a small round ball someone has pasted on her body. Suddenly she hisses, I am going to lock you in a cupboard if you don't stop eating that peanut butter. I stop, midspoon. Our mother laughs. You'll feel better in a few months, she tells Sadia.

Sadia as Adviser (II): At school, I study very hard and when I come home, I eat meals with my parents. Sometimes some of the girls ask me if I'd like to practice long jumps, but I resolutely say no. I do not want to give people the impression that I will follow in Sadia's footsteps. She has already done everything a woman is expected to do and those are very high expectations to live up to. Sometimes, Sadia calls me in the evenings and asks me how I'm doing, she wants to gossip about our teachers, but I give her noncommittal answers. Everything is exactly how you left it. She sighs, says, Don't get married, and I think of the vastness of my life, marked as it is by the absence of men.

Sadia as Coffee Drinker: The one thing Sadia won't give up during pregnancy is coffee. She drinks two cups a day and maintains it will be fine for the baby. Our mother cries and pleads with her to stop. Sadia is serene. She says, I won't. She is like a bitter gourd stuck to a vine, finally able to wave blissfully against our mother now that she is also almost a mother. I work on graduate college applications in the evenings.

Sadia as Mother: Sadia calls me crying two months after the birth of her daughter. It is 3:00 a.m. and I am awake because I have just started working as a journalist at a twenty-four-seven private news outlet. She asks through real sobs, Was I as boring a daughter as my daughter? I remind her of the story of her birth and she says, A black day indeed and hangs up.

Sadia as Divorcée: Sadia says nothing has happened though we all question her closely about ropes and weights and the harm they can do to the body of a woman when used by a man. At work, my boss says I have to look at the heart of a story and report from its eye. As a family, we examine Sadia's eyes for the heart. She seems okay. She says over and over again, as if she is in a perpetual state of surprise, He's just such an average guy. Our mother looks at her afraid, asks over and over again in retaliation, Is that really what your problem is?

Sadia as Villain: Sadia's husband's parents come over and weep, Sadia's husband comes over and weeps. They think there is a ghost in her. Nobody understands her discontent. Before Sadia moves back in, I email the admissions offices of the universities where I have been admitted, tell them I will need to decline their offers. They write back and urge me to defer for a year, see how I feel in another semester. Sadia and I sleep on the king-size bed together with the baby. One night she whispers, It's all the coffee and we both begin to laugh.

Sadia as Possessed: A lady who is renowned in certain circles for being fluent in the language of God comes over. She takes Sadia into the drawing room and asks her to lie down with her shirt off. My mother and I stand there too. I close my fist around the Swiss Army knife. Just in case. The lady says some verses over Sadia's back, sprinkles holy water on her. We all pray for her to come to her senses. After the lady leaves, Sadia calmly puts her shirt back on, reaches up with her hands so my mother can give her back the baby, and says, I still want a divorce. I want so badly to be possessed by her clarity that I almost die.

Sadia as Driver: Sadia starts learning how to drive. She says now that she lives at home again she needs basic skills. We learn together, take turns on the street outside our house, venturing farther and farther every day. Soon, we start taking the baby out. Our father says, You will all get killed. We eat at a restaurant close to our house, leaving the car doors unlocked, heady on freedom.

Sadia as Impetus: One Sunday, on the way home, her eyes on the road, Sadia tells me that I need to start experiencing my own life. The words come out of nowhere, as things often do in the middle of fine spring days. I want to die of shame. A month later, I open those applications again, write back to see if there is a way to convert the *Defer* to an *Accept* and start in the fall. They all write back with emails that start with *Congratulations!*

Sadia as Catalyst: I tell the family over lunch one afternoon that I have been accepted into the graduate program of journalism at UC Berkeley. Sadia is twenty-eight and I am twenty-six. It's because of you, I tell her, trying to smile. When I look into her eyes, I see that she remembers the words she flung in the car that day. I am gratified when she looks away first, turns instead to the child bawling by her hip. It occurs to me that my sister might be scared of who she will be if I am no longer who I have always been.

Sadia as Opposer: For days, I start sentences with *At UC Berkeley*—and at first Sadia smiles, but then more and more I notice she leaves the room when I talk about leaving for America. One day, when I am telling her about how I have to sign up for my elective classes exactly a week before they begin and no sooner and no later, she suddenly bursts, Will you please be quiet? There are more important things in life! I'm sorry, she says to my hurt face and my parents' surprised faces. The child says something and we all look at her, grateful for the distraction.

Sadia as Stopper: I lie in bed with Sadia, her daughter between us like a plant. I think Sadia is asleep until I hear her suddenly speak. Please stay, she says. It is almost a whisper and she does not repeat herself. And suddenly, I remember all those years ago when she was trying to marry the boy. I need her to be on my side now and let me learn to hold myself in other permutations of love. I keep my breathing even so it seems like I'm already asleep. In the morning, she doesn't bring it up again. It doesn't feel so bad after all, carving this space out for myself in the face of her need.

Sadia as Vicarious Student: At UC Berkeley, all the roofs are shingled red. A boy at the orientation walks up to me and says, This just *in*, I'm *Justin*, and shows me all his teeth. Later, on the phone, I tell Sadia, who says, Did you remember to pack the Swiss Army knife?

Sadia as Injured Person: Another thing that comes out of nowhere: My father calls when I have only been in America for three weeks and says, Your mother was sitting in the front seat with Sadia's daughter on her lap. Sadia was driving. The taxi appeared and the two cars made contact. He lists out the coordinates of the accident over the crackling phone line. I have trouble listening because all I can think is, Oh this big thing is finally happening to my life and I am not even there for it. And I think of Sadia's eyes in the car, a person all their own, wide and terrified at the idea of living on in the body of a mother who is witnessing the death of her child. I think of my father pacing circles in the hospital waiting room going Ya Allah Reham down the phone line. I ask if I should come back, and he says, Wait until we know more. I know that even if he said, Yes come back, I could not bring myself to go back to the scene of a disaster. One look, and I might get stuck inside it.

Sadia as Absence (IV): My father calls again and says, The baby and your mother are fine, only a few minor scratches, but Sadia has still not woken up. He will keep me up to date. My mother only weeps on the phone when he gives the phone to her. I start to wear my phone around my neck like a talisman, leave it on vibrate so when anyone calls it feels like my heart has jump-started against my chest. I try to go to classes. In my Conflict in the Middle East course Sadia yells in my head, her mouth bloody after the accident, Pakistan is my mother! Shut up, I yell at the walls when I get home, that doesn't even make sense.

Sadia as Critic: Justin invites me to his house and I accept for want of a distraction. The two of us stand near the fridge and he leans into me. I turn my face a little to the side. Sorry, he says, it's just that you did come over, and I nod. *It's hard to argue with facts* is the mantra of journalism students everywhere. I did come over, I repeat, before leaving. Sadia could be dead, I say out loud when I'm walking home. In my head, Sadia confirms that I'm right; Good job stating the facts, she says, rasping for breath. It occurs to me that if I do everything she doesn't want me to do, maybe she will live to spite me. When I get home, I call Justin and invite him over to my house.

Sadia as Admonisher: Justin comes over late that very night and sits at the dining table with me. Sadia is there too. We talk for a long time about classes. He believes the Middle East has intractable problems. Those are his exact words, *intractable problems*, and he looks closely at me to make sure I am on board with this. I'm Pakistani, I tell him, shrugging. Dead Sadia rolls her eyes. Justin asks if he can spend the night on the couch, and even though his house is close by and there is no reason for him to stay, I say, Yes. He's going to keep asking until he's in your bed, my sister warns me.

Sadia as Survivor: Three weeks after the accident, Dead Sadia wakes up. I imagine my parents have spent every day waiting blankly in the hospital waiting room with animal looks on their faces. Later, my mother tells me that before the doctor told them the good news, she said to him, Sadia's daughter is young, like a plea. The doctor explained it to them, Sadia's eyes jerked backward and forward in her head with the car during the accident. He says she might have trouble seeing. Maybe for a while. Maybe forever. Later, when she is able to, Sadia speaks to me on the phone, croaks, Thank God my daughter is safe, as if she has rehearsed her reaction to finding out she could be blind.

Sadia as Celebration: I go to a party that night to celebrate. A boy called Brian spills wine on my clothes. When Justin comes over to help, Brian drunkenly puts an arm around Justin's shoulder and says to me, He likes them exotic, doesn't he, our friend?

They both beam but I stare at them so they become uncomfortable. Finally, I walk away. That night Justin texts me: *I'm sorry*, say the words on my phone, *You're teaching me to be a better person*. *Ok*, I text back and then block him.

Sadia as Mirror: Sadia and I have the same eyes yes, but my nose is longer and sharper, and my forehead smaller, I have some weight on my upper arms.

Sadia as Blind Woman: When she comes home from the hospital, Sadia calls me and says, Every day I am going to thank God for saving my daughter. Still, when my mother takes the phone from her, she tells me Sadia is fumbling to pour milk, fumbling to lift her daughter, fumbling to even walk from room to room without bumping into chairs and lamps.

Sadia as Phoning It In: Here is the trajectory of blindness over a year: First, my older sister says, I am so glad my daughter is alive. Second, she says, I wish I could see. Third, she says, I'm so angry everyone survived except me.

Sadia as Cheerleader: Sadia calls less and less, and then not at all. On my one-year anniversary in America I dream that she is standing spotlit on a stage. Around her my eyes gleam. In my dream, guilt is a real cockroach eating at my insides but Sadia steps on it, squashes my internal organs, says, You should have come back! What are you doing over there except trying to catch up with all the life I've already lived! Here in this other country, I resolve to make people who don't know me love only me.

Sadia as Sexpert: One night after class, and two weeks before I go back home to visit, I find Brian-friend-of-Justin. I say, I'd like to have sex. I push the words out before I have the time to think. I can't go back as the same person I was when I left. Sadia lost her eyes, and I still have nothing to show for mine. Not even something as basic as a penis! I've never slept with a woman from another country before, he says. I don't tell him I've never slept with anyone except for Sadia before, because that would be weird.

Sadia as Amused Audience: After undressing me, Brian asks if I am sure. Yes, I nod. He leans toward his wallet, pulls out a condom, and presses it on while I appear disinterested. I think, This smells like plastic. That's when Sadia appears in my head. In a taunting voice she jumbles her sentences, No one can hurt us and I don't kiss and tell, but boy that first night was good. Brian positions himself on top of me, kisses my shoulder. I thought for sure you were fucking Justin this past year, he says. Sadia finally speaks up. Red flag, she says, and I am so relieved that she is still here, I say, I think we should stop. Brian lifts himself off me a little. His mouth opens and closes before he arranges his features into a look of concern. He says, If your parents had you sewn shut, you can tell me. He's scared when I begin to laugh, sits up with his back to me, gets dressed quickly and leaves.

Sadia as Stranger: They are all waiting in the doorway when my airport taxi pulls up to the house at the start of July. Sadia's daughter pulls away because she does not recognize me anymore. Sadia is a little thinner and stares right through me when she hugs me. I do not know what to do with my body so my parents engulf me in their arms, my father tears up a little. Later, over lunch, my parents say they have been waiting to surprise me, Sadia got some good news today! The doctor has told her that her ophthalmology x-rays seem to be showing some improvement. That night, Sadia and I lie awake for a long time without speaking. Finally I say, I'm sorry, and I am grateful that my voice doesn't break as I say it. She scoffs, says, What about? When I don't reply she says, a little gentler this time, I didn't expect you to hang around me forever. The sentence soaks up the room. Speaking of hanging out, I finally say, and begin to tell her about Brian. He smelled a bit like American cleaning products, I end. She holds her stomach while she laughs, tears fall down her cheeks and I think I will never feel happier than at this moment. Finally, we both fall silent again. She says, Maybe he would have done the dishes every day though. I look at her. She shrugs. I hear men there like doing the dishes. We fall asleep giggling.

Sadia as Patient: Our mother tells Sadia she needs to look at the color green to continue healing her eyes. I drive her to the trails near the Margalla Hills one day. We sit at the foot of the hills, facing the forest, as whole families move past us to spread across the mountains. We stare and stare at the leaves of trees, craning our necks, sometimes talking, most often not. While we sit there, Sadia brings a leaf closer and farther from her face over and over again. She says, You know before you left I asked you to stay, and I know you heard me. When I look at her, her face is empty of any expression. My stomach coils in on itself. If she asks me to stay now, I know I will. A little boy stands by a car in the parking lot near the entrance to the trails, trying to pull open a car door. She sighs. I'm proud of you, she says. I'll miss you when you leave again.

Sadia as Sister: The night before my flight back to America, my mother lies down with Sadia, her daughter, and me, and into the child's ear she half laughs, half whispers the story of what happened when she brought me back from the hospital the afternoon of my birth. She says our father leaned down to show my face to Sadia, and before he could stop her, Sadia leaned in and darted out her small pink tongue. She licked my face all the way from my temple to my mouth. I want to taste what I taste like, she said by way of explanation, when our father snatched me back. The room is awash in the soft, pale-green light from the glow-in-the-dark stars pasted on the ceiling as my mother speaks and Sadia and I reach for each other's hands to the sound of her voice. Tomorrow, I will fly back to where I live, and over the course of our lives, the endings will arrive for us again and again, and each time, demand to be welcomed with open arms. Nobody has taught me that living a life that is entirely your own is also an act of mourning.

BASIC TRAINING

Two months ago, our mother was admitted to the Noor Hospital for People Who Need Organs and New Teeth. My sister and I had just finished donating blood and were in the parking lot of the hospital, both of us sitting in our car with the doors open, taking great gulping breaths of fresh air to restore our energy. Around us, paramedics leaped out of screaming ambulances and tried stretching soldiers back to life. A young man in a blue kameez and a red sash leaned over a stretcher, his cheeks like small hard tumors in his face. He gently admonished the soldier, This is selfish, guy, pull yourself together, while his friend stood next to him taking quick, worried puffs from a joint.

A man walked up to us as we exhaled together, our heads between our knees. Sisters, he said, you look tired. We closed the doors against him and started to reverse out of there. When we were midway home we rolled down the windows and started talking about the special hatred we'd developed for little children. We agreed that now we saw them for what they really were (useless).

My sister and I determinedly refused to acknowledge the kids living on our street. They held balls, bats, dolls, chalk, twigs, badminton rackets, clods of dirt, prams of younger siblings, the corners of their mothers' clothes, their own arms and legs. They looked torn and used up, unspooling on the streets. Their parents orbited terraces above them, one eye on the children, the other on God knows what. Raheel Sb, next door, was a retired major and fancied himself a catcher of spies in these times of war. When he walked on his terrace, he kept his binoculars trained on the homeless uncle sitting cross-legged outside the general store. The store was famous for deep-frying its potato wedges and serving them up in oiled scraps of newspaper. When we drove back from the hospital that day, the sun was going down and the street smelled stale and salty. Mosquitoes the size of our fists flew in the air and splattered themselves against our windshield. Raheel Sb pointed his binoculars at us once and then moved them away.

The man in the parking lot was back when we visited our mother in the hospital a week later. Our kameezes stuck to us because of the heat. I had just donated my hair; my sister had sacrificed a finger. There is another way for you to contribute to the war effort without giving of yourself quite so literally, he said, assuming that we were donating to the soldiers. Despite feeling out of sorts because of the sudden dearth of young men in the country, we ignored him. We recognized a line when we heard one. Driving home, we looked at how the women walking on the sides of the road clutched their clothes closer to their bodies in a way that was both extremely modest and very attractive to the boys growing up in the area (who had their pick now that their older brothers were dead or soon to be dead).

The third time we drove out to see our mother we could not stand it. We did not even go inside the hospital. Our hair lapped at our chins. While we were sitting there, the man came to our window and asked us to come with him. The wind picked up and tunneled inside our car and tried getting into our eyes. The hospital's walls disappeared against our lashes. Perhaps two or four more people had died inside—hopefully and God forbid though, not our mother. The man had a small mustache, so dark it almost looked blue, and small, bright-brown eyes. He was wearing a white linen vest and a light black blazer. His name was Rafi and he needed us, he said. We are done being needed, we told him. It felt good to say it out loud. The hospital came back into focus. Not like that, he replied. You girls have egos!

We were so embarrassed by the immodesty of our thinking that we didn't say anything when he got into the back seat of our car. A man with such small hands cannot be harmful, we tried telling each other telepathically, with our backs straight against our seats and my sister's knuckles tight around the car's steering wheel. We were right; he didn't pull out guns and simply directed us around corners and down narrow alleys. Eventually we turned onto a road far away from anywhere we had ever driven. One side of this road was lined by a high concrete wall that went on for quite a while. The other looked out into rows and rows of great oak trees. We parked before a small metallic gate. Rafi banged the inside of his palm flat against the metal and yelled, Oi!

We heard scratching behind the door. A head appeared over the top of the wall, a messy little boy, his face swollen and confused, as if he had just been beaten up, or had been asleep. He dropped out of sight again. We heard someone drawing back bolts.

The gate opened and we were led into a large field, grassy in patches. There were hundreds of little boys and girls. Large men wearing bright purple stood in the four corners of the walled area holding black rifles. The youngest of the children is three, Rafi told us proudly, the oldest is ten. Next to the gate was a raised wooden platform. Rafi also pointed out large black speakers, one in each corner. Of course we had heard that they were picking up homeless children and training them for the cause. But the children were not in Technicolor the way they had been in our heads. They were feral and dusty. The girls wore brown frocks that came down to their feet. The boys wore long brown robes.

Someone had taken a branch and gouged out lines in the grass so the field was divided into five identical-looking squares. Each square holds forty children, Rafi said. In the distance, we saw a man in purple take aim and shoot a small girl who had been crying loudly. The air cracked and she fell to the ground like a mannequin. The children around her paused for a second and then backed away like performers in a circus, young and taut. They seemed full of rage, as if directly feeding on the heat from the sun. One girl elbowed a gap-toothed little boy in the stomach. The toy grenade he had been playing with went flying. He lunged at her face with open hands until her lips started to bleed. My sister and I were only small scale sinners. Like when the paramedics laid our mother out in the ambulance and instead of feeling scared we were annoyed. When she screamed, it was a long, shining sound that soared straight to the roof of our skulls.

Rafi climbed onto the wooden platform. The men in purple began to walk away. Rafi picked up a megaphone and spoke into it, his voice echoing around the field. He said, The ants are here—this directed at the children and accompanied by a short, flat wink at us. At first we thought we were the ants and glanced, insulted, down at our clothes as if we were late and poorly grown, but then we noticed that the roar of the children was directed at the reentering men who were now holding big gray buckets as they walked back onto the field.

We start them off small, Rafi explained to us. Yesterday it was ladybugs followed by sedated squirrels. Today it's ants and tomorrow it's kittens. We move on to the human enemy next week. The men grimaced as they pulled buckets in through the gate. The ants—fire ants, we noticed with admiration—climbed over the handles of the buckets and bit their hands. The children ran to the men. They overturned the buckets and the ground crawled orange. It shook from so many small feet jumping in the air. Their stamping drummed into our heads like a song. We sweated with fear and heat. When all the ants were dead, the children continued scooping them into their hands. They tried to crush them into a fine red powder. It's protein, we heard one small boy woozily tell a girl who could only have been his sister. He had welts the size of boulders on his arms and legs.

We left for home when the children began to breathe normally again. We told Rafi we would be back tomorrow, perhaps in the evening. We are not ready yet, we said, implying, we later realized, that we would be ready soon.

At the hospital the next day our mother asked us about our lives and we told her about what we had seen. She laughed and called us her silly dolls. The secret made us feel happy and bloated, as if our insides finally matched our outsides. A nurse came in to help with the daily exercises. She lifted our mother's arms and legs carefully, one by one, as if she was a banana leaf and the hospital was inspecting her for holes.

Outside our mother's room, we noticed a little girl in the corridor. In our defense, she looked very bored. She must have been six. My sister bent down to her level and asked for her name and she told us it was Asya. We hadn't spoken to any children in months. We exchanged looks and asked Asya if she wanted to come with us for a ride while she waited, and she said yes, very shyly, her thumb and forefinger playing with a blue bead. In the parking lot, she squinted against the late evening sun and in the car she put her head out of the back window while we drove. Her hair fluttered against her face and she screamed into the wind to tell us that her brother had been sick forever. We felt very bad for her and almost turned back. But children are shaped by the shape of their country. In the long term, we consoled ourselves, we weren't really doing any harm.

Asya was frightened and unsmiling by the time we led her into the grounds. Someone had turned the stadium lights on. Rafi's smile was too huge, his teeth like cracked white bones in his mouth. He held out his hand to the little girl, and she took it. We noticed she kept the hand with the bead clutched into a fist.

She began to cry when Rafi urged her nicely—to his credit—to join the children in the center square. We begged him to wait for just a little while. He seemed resigned as he nodded. The sooner the better, he warned, and we agreed in principle. We led Asya to the center block and sat with her on the grass, asked her to show us her bead, though she did not. The children were busy with a kitten activity. The men in the field kept reentering through the metal gate holding pink, furless bodies that looked like rats. A four-year-old grabbed at one of the small animals a man set by her feet and held it up to her face. Its small paws wound in the air and it let out short, sharp cries. The girl scrunched up her face in concentration and tightened her grip around the kitten's neck. Rafi's mustache hair waved in apology. Some children found pieces of rope left over from previous exercises and fashioned nooses. One boy with a dark mole at the place where his eyebrow ended crushed a kitten with his foot so it lay splashed against the grass like a dark red clot. They continued like this until the sound of crying faded from the air.

We sat with Asya while all of this was happening until someone cut off the area's electricity and the field plunged into darkness. One of the men started a small fire in our square and some of the children wrapped themselves around its edges. A few children who were farther away edged closer to the fire. We saw a boy look both ways and cross the line that led from his block into ours before he was shot by a purple man.

Asya was the only one wearing a yellow dress, and the other children looked at her, ravenous. One little boy tried to rip it off so we punched him in his face. She began to cry again, and we got a little tired of her. Look, we said, trying to get her to smile. We hopped on one leg and then another, waved our hands around her face, stuck our fingers in our mouths and pulled them into wide grins. Some of the other children copied us. Mosquitoes hummed in the air and we heard planes approaching in the distance. The heat from the fire burned into our skin.

Panicking, we did the dance our mother had taught us when we were children. We spun as gracefully as we could. The children began to form lines behind us, straining their eyes to see, stumbling and laughing as they tried to keep up in the dark. Rafi watched from what seemed like far away, perhaps too tired to move closer, perhaps too slow to realize what was happening. Asya stopped crying and used her nails to dig out a small hole in the ground. She put her bead in it carefully before standing to join us. The night smelled like water and grass. I should not have to string these scenes up in front of you like this to help you understand that the word *loss* has a weight that cannot be borne. We saw two children begin to kiss each other like adults by the fire and strained to ignore our hearts, finally beginning to beat, large and fearful, in our mouths.

THE FUNERAL

Yesterday I went to my aunt's funeral. She was my father's older sister. Long before he died we lost touch with her and my uncle and their sons. Small misunderstandings arose and then they became bigger, until decades had wedged themselves between our families. She had two boys. Every summer, I had begged them to let me play cricket with them. They never said yes, though sometimes they let my brothers play.

At her funeral I saw her two sons again—now men—sitting with bowed heads by her body. From the other guests, I heard that the doctors had said a clot had traveled from her lung all the way to her heart, stopping the flow of blood. Her oldest son was fifty-four now. I had never met his children though I think one of them was the young teenage girl carrying cups of tea back and forth from the kitchen, occasionally bending to receive pats on the back from visiting mourners. My cousins rose to greet me and my mother, and for a second we were all bemused. My mother held my dead aunt's sons—my cousins—and cried. I occasionally sniffed but wasn't able to summon tears. Both cousins had grown up handsome, tall with strong jawlines, their mother's lips trembling on their faces.

I had been told my aunt did not like my mother; that had been the root cause of my father's fight with his sister, and so I examined my mother too, who was small in the room, the corners of her mouth turned down. I wondered if my cousins thought my mother was dramatic as she cried, after all, she had not seen them in years. Perhaps she was sad for herself, or sad in the way people are when they realize the end is coming and all the people they have known in their lives are marching in a line toward the edge of the cliff, falling off one by one. The smell of rice cooking wafted through the house. We had also heard that my aunt had been diagnosed with Alzheimer's. During the last two years she had forgotten how to eat, and so there had been a tube in her stomach through which they fed her mush three times a day. She had even forgotten how to talk. Another thing we heard: many years ago, when her older son married and brought his wife home, she had made the woman stand and pray in the center of the room in her wedding clothes and loudly criticized her form until the new bride burst into tears.

Yesterday, on the way to the funeral, my mother had said, God never forgives some things, and I wondered if she was thinking about this story. But this daughter-in-law, now wedded for many years to the older son, was at the funeral, fine lines around her mouth, holding a boy to her side. Maybe he was seven or eight. Even the woman's mother, the boy's grandmother, was there, and the three of them looked like carbon copies of one another as they spoke in low voices among the other guests.

My aunt's husband, my uncle, was old, almost eighty-seven, and was beginning to forget things too. While I stood in the room trying to pay my condolences to him, another man moved in front of me to say, We are so sorry for your loss, may Allah grant her Jannah.

And my uncle replied, Oh she was so young, only fifty-seven.

The other man said loudly, She was eighty-five. He had the air of a man who was compelled to restore order, and I was grateful. I felt afraid suddenly that I would leave here with the number fifty-seven lodged in my brain and later, when my mother died, my mind would trick me into comforting myself by thinking, Oh at least she lived longer than my aunt.

No, no, my uncle said. She was fifty-seven.

The other man replied firmly, She was eighty-five.

Finally my uncle looked around the room and, spotting me, asked, Are you eighty-five?

At this my cousins rose from the body's side and said, Abu, come with us, and led him out of the room. When we were kids, the younger one used to eat mayonnaise out of jars because everyone thought it was funny. At mealtimes whenever we were together, his mother would hand him a jar of mayonnaise after he had eaten his meal and he would open it, dip his finger in, and lick it clean while we all laughed and his mother shook her head as if she did not know what to do with him.

This aunt had not come to the funeral for my father, her own brother. We later heard she was telling people that she had not gone because she knew my mother would not let her in, though she should not have worried—all that day my mother had been preoccupied, glancing at the corners of the living room where we were receiving mourners. My father, in his last days, had started dictating wishes for his burial and the wake. Now she wanted to remember exactly how he'd phrased each wish. She thought the people who had come to pay their respects somehow knew that she was in the process of forgetting. Weeks later she kept asking me, Did so-and-so say anything?

Now my younger cousin came back to where I was standing and spoke to me in a low voice. What are you doing these days? I had heard he was not married. I was surprised to note he had a thin, plaintive voice. I told him I wasn't doing much, as if we were old friends and we were just catching up after a week of not speaking. He nodded and looked around, distracted.

She jumped off the roof, he said.

Startled, I looked over my shoulder as if she had jumped off the roof simply to reappear behind me. She couldn't walk, I reminded him gently, wondering if grief had addled his brain.

She could, he said. He spoke a little louder than he had intended. People turned to look at us. He smiled at my forehead, as if to reassure the room that things were okay. Then he looked directly at me and said, Anyway, what would you know?

She jumped off the roof, I repeated. He nodded, patted my shoulder. It's good to tell someone that, he said. His chin trembled.

In the other room, my uncle was loudly saying to everyone who would listen, I keep telling everyone she was fifty-seven, maybe fifty-eight, and I could hear loud hmms of agreement.

My cousin moved away and I peeked into the room my uncle was speaking in. When my aunt was still alive, someone must have taken care of the couple, reminded him to take his medicine, bathed and fed my aunt when she forgot to do it herself. I saw people exchanging looks as if my aunt had been the one keeping the whole family together and now that she was dead, they were witnessing its impending dissolution in real time. What will happen to this old man now?

I tried to think of ways to love her. I remembered that when I was a child, we had all been watching TV and she had changed the channel when a commercial for sanitary napkins had come on. Then she looked at my mother and said, When we were young, this never would have been on TV, and when I asked her what that meant, she laughed. I imagined her laughing, flying off the roof on a sanitary napkin, yelling, Look how times have changed!

My other cousin, the older one, came up behind me and said, Actually Junaid wasn't feeling that well when he said that. And minds sometimes go where you don't want them to. I couldn't tell if he was talking about his brother's mind or his mother's mind or his own. I looked back to see where my younger cousin was standing in the corner. The two brothers exchanged a look I couldn't decipher.

Of course, I said.

When I thought of my own brothers, who lived far away and were married, I wanted to always love them. Sometimes when they called after weeks of not calling, I picked up the phone anyway to talk to them because I remembered how when my father was dying, you could see in the way his body was becoming just some bones that he wanted to be held together by people who had known the shape of him as a child.

After my older cousin walked away to greet some guests, Junaid motioned for me to follow him. He led me to the kitchen where a cook was stirring a big spoon into a pot. Chicken? the cook murmured as I passed, and I shook my head. A door from the kitchen led onto the lawn. From there, Junaid and I walked out to the main gate. He walked me all the way around the wall bordering the house until we were facing the back of the house.

It was all dirt. He pointed to the ground, where you could see a small patch. It looked maroon, like it could have been sheep blood, or goat blood, or almost black, like water from sewers had hardened and crusted there. This is where she landed, he said. He looked directly at me. As one, we looked at the roof. I began to believe it.

I just couldn't take it anymore, he said.

How did she—?

I helped.

You lifted her over the railing?

Yes.

I wondered then if he could kill me too. As if he could read my mind, he quietly said, I just needed someone to know who had known her when she was in her right mind.

I nodded.

He let out a low laugh. I loved her but she could be mean sometimes.

I thought of the jars of mayonnaise and his strained smile as he licked his little fingers clean, and I nodded again.

I'm sorry about your father, he said.

He wanted to live, I said. I wanted him to know there was a difference between our parents. When nearing the end, my father had begun to celebrate small achievements, like being able to walk on certain days. But still he had succumbed to death quietly, the only obvious sign of objection the deep, rattling breaths he took on his final day that clanged in my skull for weeks after we buried him. What was the difference between them now that they were both dead?

As if he understood, Junaid nodded. She asked me to do it. She was so sick.

With my foot I scuffed the dirt and moved it around. The color began to disappear.

You're okay, I replied, as if saying the words would put him back together. I remembered then that I had said those words to my father when he was in the hospital and needed blood drawn, needed a new test, got some bad news. I realized now that I missed saying those words, that I wanted to repeat them forever to everyone I had ever known. I was afraid I would grow old and not know anyone willing to say them back to me.

Yes, he replied, I'm okay. Can I call you sometimes?

Before I could agree, we began to hear people calling his name in the house so we made our way back inside. His older brother glared at us as we entered.

The men picked up the body to carry it outside and eventually to the graveyard. Junaid started to make a loud keening sound as soon as they lifted her. She jumped, he said loudly. She really, really jumped. I helped her, he said. I dropped her in one go. Everyone shushed him as they carried the body out the door. You could tell they wanted to bury her quickly, smooth the earth over this whole day so everyone could go back to their routines. Under the ground there was my father and soon my aunt and one day it would be this son, who was wailing loudly as he got into the ambulance with the body, I pulled the tube out of her stomach and lifted her! Everyone shook their heads. Those boys really loved their mother, I heard a woman whisper to another woman.

After the men took my aunt's body to the graveyard, I finally went and sat in the big lounge where all the women were sitting. My mother was already there and she made space for me next to her and for just one moment I felt like I had when I was a child and wanted to be near her all the time. I looked around the room, at all the people and distant relatives my aunt had collected in her lifetime. It surprised me that she had continued to deserve and receive generosity from people even during all those years we were estranged. My father used to say, The point of life is to collect people to come to your funeral. These people would not come to my mother's funeral.

There was an older woman there and she was snoring on the sofa. I took off my shoes and put my handbag to the side. My mother and I began to read from the Quran. My aunt's grandchildren came in and out of the room, and the women spoke in low voices about their daily lives. Some of them knew my name even though I had never seen them before. They said, How are you? Good, I replied.

Suddenly I was very exhausted. Like the old woman on the sofa, I just wanted to sleep. The men began to come back. They looked tired, and their shoes were caked in dust from where they had stood around the grave when my aunt's body was lowered into it. Junaid was quiet now. He came in and went straight upstairs to his room. I knew then that I would never see him again.

Every year, my aunt's family had visited or we had visited them during the long summer holidays in June, July, and August. My brothers and our two cousins and I had spent the days jostling for space on a sofa while playing Nintendo, only stopping for food. For dessert we kept blocks of ice cream in the freezer. They came packaged in long rectangles of cardboard. If we left the ice cream sitting out too long, it would begin to leak out of the cardboard's edges. My mother would bring an ice cream block out after every meal, and all of us would watch as she quickly used a knife to cut the smooth rectangle into even pieces for us. We held out our bowls where she dropped our share in. After that, my father and my aunt would begin to argue about what would go best with the ice cream and for a few moments, the rest of us had a feeling that they had forgotten us. Cornflakes, coconut shavings, packets of crisps, french fries. They would put something different into every bowl, and then we would pass them around the table so everyone could vote on what tasted the best. Usually my aunt's choices of what went best with ice cream won, and then she would beam for the rest of the night. Now I think my father let her win. It was a wonderful thing when she smiled. There are many things we take to our graves just because there is no language for how to recount the experience of having lived through them.

Finally my mother motioned for me to get up; it was time for us to go home. From the window, I could see it was a new moon that night, a lovely spring evening. I moved my foot absently as if to find my shoe. It touched leather and I looked down and saw I had put my foot into my handbag. I glanced around quickly to make sure that no one was watching, but the old woman was awake now and she was watching. What an idiot, she said loudly, and then she began to laugh. It took only a second for everyone to see what she was laughing at, and then suddenly the room was alight with laughter. I was prepared to feel hurt but it felt gentle and edifying; that whole evening I had felt like I was walking on something fragile and finally that thing had broken, and now my mother and I were falling through air. All our relatives, all these people we had not seen for years, held us aloft for a bit as they must have done when my parents were younger and when I was a child, and then finally the laughter died, and we were on our way.

THE NEWLYWEDS

The girl's mother said the man would make a woman out of her. Three nights before the wedding she said, Listen, I want to tell you something. There was a long pause. After the conversation, the mother left, shuffling her feet as she went as if ready to turn back any second. It had been a hard, hot day, and the girl boiled on her bed. She called her best friend that same evening and asked her to sleep over. At night, the two friends crept into her sleeping brother's room to find the DVDs, holding their hands over their mouths to keep from laughing. Then they tiptoed back to the girl's room and waited.

The parents' bedroom door clicked shut, and the sound of the father's snores rose and fell like a tide through the house. Finally, the girl opened one of the DVD cases, and her heart beat faster at what was inside: the image of a man and a woman embracing, unclothed, the man's face buried in the woman's chest as if he were hungry or dead.

The friends muted the volume on the television before pressing Play. A man pushed into a woman from behind, holding onto her hips as if she were a misshapen anchor. His face stayed taut like cutlery in the small, blue-white screen. After the movie was over, the girl sat cross-legged on her bed, facing her friend. She practice whispered moaning sounds. At first they laughed, but soon they became serious about the sounds. They practiced for thirty minutes and then went to sleep.

———

The man the girl ended up marrying was careful in bed, and shy. He booked a hotel room for the wedding night, one that smelled of roses and had little chocolate hearts placed carefully on the pillows. He sat at the very edge of the bed and told her she was very pretty even before she'd stepped out of the bathroom, as if he had been practicing saying it over and over when she was inside. He stumbled over the words to get them out, looking up at the corners of the ceiling. This made her like him a little more.

Her best friend married a month after her. They met once after their weddings on the rooftop of a recently opened café. The girl wore a black kameez, covered in small, silver sequins, gold hoops in her ears. Her friend was equally dressed up, her hair cut in a new way, the bangs angling to the right, making her look permanently surprised. They felt suddenly awkward and could not talk about much, instead saying over and over again that life was so different now, and then nodding without wanting to dwell on the specifics.

When they said goodbye, kissing each other gently on the cheek like real women, the girl became conscious that distinct lines had been drawn in the short time after their weddings, containing new, still-unknown loyalties. Perhaps this, she later thought, was what made a woman: this easy shifting into new mental territory when it came to other people.

———

The girl, now a woman, had been living with the man in the new neighborhood for only three months, but already she had been invited to the wives' weekly get-togethers. At the first meeting, she made it clear, after the older women asked, that it had not been a love marriage. Her voice was high, like a child's, and she spoke with a smile that came and went from her face.

This added to her growing reputation for strangeness.

It was well known in the neighborhood that the newly married couple kept a goat in their backyard. In the mornings after the man left for work the woman walked the goat up and down the street. It was not common for people to have pets but when they did, it was usually cats or dogs. The woman felt the ladies' interest keenly and was both excited and worried by it. She knew they were all waiting for her to invite them over so they could look more closely at her life.

Finally, on a stifling Tuesday near the end of June, while at Mrs. Rashida's place, the young woman offered her place as the next point of meeting. Please, she said, why don't we do the next one at my house? As usual, she spoke in an enthusiastic voice, leaning forward toward the food as she spoke, clasping her hands to her chest in a gesture of sincerity the rest of them would make fun of later. Mrs. Rashida accepted for all the women in the room. That will be really nice, she said. Upstairs, a child woke and began to cry, a thin, straining sound that wove through the house. The hostess smiled apologetically, and the ladies filed out one by one, lingering at the door for a few minutes to say goodbye.

The woman told the man that same night about hosting the next get-together. He had stripped the sheets off the bed, saying it was cooler that way. She could feel the slight ribs of the mattress under her back as they talked.

What will you cook? He turned his neck so that he was looking at her, wearing a white vest and shorts whose ends fluttered a little under the fan.

I don't know, maybe fruit with some yogurt would be nice in this weather.

They had opened the windows before getting into bed, and hot air came in through the screens and settled on their bodies. The goat bleated once and then was silent. They were still new enough in the marriage to believe that going to bed without sex was a sign that something was wrong. She allowed him to kiss her and reached for the small, blue-green towel she kept near the bed. She laid it out under herself first. She guessed she could grow to like the way he kissed her mouth, chastely almost, as if asking for permission.

On the afternoon of the party, the bell rang for the first time at 1:00 p.m. The woman was still in the kitchen cutting fruit. She had laid out the kiwis, the bananas, the apples, the mangoes, and the watermelon in front of her. It had not rained all week, and the weather had become unbearable. On hearing the bell ring, she quickly rinsed and dried her hands. It was Mrs. Anjum, her head and face covered by her dupatta to prevent sunburn. She was holding her daughter's arm up in the air, as if dragging her along. The girl was small, maybe came up to her mother's knees. You know, said Mrs. Anjum, even before saying hello, I couldn't leave her at home. Her eyes went to a congregation of young men standing on the street corner under a burst pipe that served as a makeshift fountain for the neighborhood during the summer.

Of course, said the young woman, patting the little girl's head. It's so lovely to have you both here.

Soon the other women also arrived. They all brought their daughters. Mrs. Hameed also brought her seven-year-old son. All these women and their children. Maybe there were twenty people there. That goat is so fat, said one of the women, peeking at the backyard through the door leading out from the kitchen. Yes, everyone else murmured, interested, isn't it too much work? The young woman smiled at the room. No, no, she said, I love animals. The children and the mothers stared. They looked at her china cups and the small glass cabinet. They moved their necks this way and that. The young woman wished the man would come home. He had promised to be there before the guests arrived.

I'll cook lunch, the woman said. Since your children came, you cannot leave without lunch. I'll just lay out the appetizers first. She brought out the diced fruit and the yogurt, the small plates from the kitchen. The ladies relaxed as they forked food into their mouths and brought their children to hold against their chairs. The conversation changed to the men and the water in the street. In this heat, the water will attract snakes. They rest in these pipes, you know, Mrs. Rashida said. The other women nodded. You should worry about your goat. I hear snake bites can kill them. The room laughed, and the young woman joined in after a second. She noticed the children were all paying attention to the conversation. Don't worry, she said, to a little girl near her, we'll beat back the snakes for you. The mother patted the girl's head, too.

The door lock began to jiggle. The ladies immediately stood at the sight of the man. Hello, he said, and smiled. The wife noticed with dismay that the ends of his legs were caked with dried mud. Sorry, he said, addressing the women, I had to walk through the water. How are you ladies today? He spoke like he was a showman on TV. The woman felt the other ladies taking mental pictures of this afternoon. He was a thin man, and his suit hung loosely around his shoulders. Sorry, the man said again, looking at her and she smiled back, straining the ends of her mouth to do so.

Together they went into the kitchen and closed the door behind them. I offered them lunch but look at how many children came. What happened to your pants?

I had to walk through water, he repeated. I'm sorry. He touched her shoulder. Why don't we ask the children to play with the goat? I'll cook and you can go sit with the aunties. He saw her face and corrected himself. Ladies, I meant, sorry.

He went back into the living room, muddy ends of pants still trailing the floor as he clapped his hands for the children's attention. The ladies sat up a little straighter, and the young woman went to sit in the lounge as the children were ushered outside. How good he is, they all said to the young woman, but wait till a few more months have passed. People kept saying this to her—wait for a few more months, wait for a few more months—a refrain that stayed stuck inside her head long after whoever said it had stopped speaking.

The man took out bread and cucumbers from the fridge. He fried some chicken in a pan and diced it, added mayonnaise and some ketchup. In the backyard the children, eight of them in total, surrounded the goat. The man could hear them daring one another to touch it. No, you touch it, no you first. One day the man hoped he'd have a little girl as beautiful as the woman. He hummed as he cut the crusts off the sandwiches. He poured juice into glasses, wiping his forehead as he went.

He had just walked out of the kitchen into the living room, holding a full tray, when they first heard the screaming. It was coming from the backyard. The *ah* the ladies started to say when they saw the sandwiches got caught in their throats. The woman followed the panicking mothers outside, already thinking of goat horns penetrating soft, little-girl arms and legs.

The young girls had positioned themselves on either side of the goat. They had found a rope and wrapped it around the animal's body. The goat was thrashing, one knee bent underneath it as the girls pulled from either end, their faces rapt and gleeful. What are you doing? the woman said, her voice loud and angry. For a second, in the light with her mouth twisted, the man thought she looked older than her years.

One of the little girls turned to the woman and said, We're preparing it for the snakes. A mother in the background laughed, but the sound was short and stopped almost immediately. The woman shooed the girls away, and they dropped the rope before stepping back, looking confused. Most of them were wearing jeans and sunglasses. Mrs. Anjum's daughter had a bright-green purse dangling off her shoulder. It was, the young woman would remember later, emblazoned with the word Courage. She thought they looked courageous and cruel, these young girls sweating in the sun. Envy fissioned inside her before she noticed the man at the other side of the group. Please stop, he said, not touching any of the girls but looking at them pleadingly. The girls stepped farther back. Come on, said one of the mothers from behind, a note of disapproval in her voice, and then in a lower voice, almost as an afterthought, How strong can the children be?

The man untangled the rope from the goat's body. It began to gallop, coming to a stop when reaching a wall and then running in the opposite direction again. It continued to make a panicked sound that grated at the woman's ears. Let's go inside, the man said finally, lunch is waiting.

The sandwiches were warm and soggy by the time they went in. The mayonnaise spilled out messily from the ends, and the guests had lost their appetite. Mrs. Anjum felt her daughter's forehead, pressing her hair out of the way first. You shouldn't have been in the sun for so long, she said.

Quickly, quietly, everyone ate. The guests did not talk about much and seemed even to have lost interest in the house. No one paused for long at the doorway. That was nice, they all said with quick, cold smiles, you have a lovely husband. The woman stood in the doorway as her guests walked away in a big group, chatting to one another, their children skipping ahead. She had the feeling that if she did not watch the ladies go home they would continue the party elsewhere, at someone else's house. A small lump rose in her throat, and she took a big breath before going inside. She went straight to the kitchen, planning to clean before resting. You were helpful today, she called to her husband, wiping the crumbs from the counter onto her hands. It took a great effort to speak. She dusted her hands off in the backyard, looking at the goat, which was standing against a wall, calmer now.

The man had already gone into the bedroom, changed, showered, and lain down to rest. Thank you, the woman repeated, standing in the doorway to the bedroom. And then, after a moment, I don't think I'm going to have the ladies over again. For the first time since they had married she sat down on his side of the bed.

She leaned in to kiss his neck, and he responded almost immediately, bringing his arms up to pull her down next to him.

Those women are old anyway, he said, kissing the side of her jaw, I'm sorry you didn't have fun.

She relaxed a little more. Did you see their faces? she asked.

Whose? He breathed the question through his mouth, his nose gently touching the bottom of her ear.

The little girls.

Yes, he said, they were monsters.

The man and the woman laughed, and the sound expanded hopefully in the room. Time stretched as they touched each other, less cautiously than before, and the smell of heat and of water on the hot, hot street came in through the windows to ground them in their new home.

Afterward, they both became drowsy and the woman dreamed she was old. In her dream she said to the man, I'm old now, and he looked at her like he'd looked at her in the sun, right before they had saved the goat together. But soon her dream changed and then changed again and when she woke she could not remember it at all.

The sun had gone down by the time she woke and slipped on her shoes and tiptoed out of the room. The man was still sleeping. She went to the backyard and tied the rope around the goat's neck. It stood still for her, trusting and calm. She slipped out the gate and walked it down the street. Water streamed out and up from the burst pipe some way down.

There were no men there anymore, all of them having left with the sound of the evening prayers. The goat pushed a foot down on the concrete street, and she led it to the water. The men had left shopping bags and discarded juice boxes around the pipe. There was even a shirt lying there, small and wet in a shallow pool. The goat moved around the water, not wanting to step directly underneath its flow, but the woman hadn't felt cold water on her body for a long time, almost since before the start of the summer. She stepped underneath the stream and felt a calmness descend.

She only turned away from the water when she heard a movement near the wall, and she hugged her arms to her chest. She remembered the snakes. The wall was tall and threw a long shadow on the street, one that almost reached her. She noticed two teenage boys sitting astride it, staring back.

Dripping, she walked back home. The man was awake by then. What happened? he asked, looking her up and down, voice still hoarse from sleep.

I went to stand under the water from the pipe. And then when he seemed worried, she quickly added, Didn't you say I was young and should have fun just before going to sleep? She tried to inject something new in her voice, something playful and teasing. The man took in her wet hair and clothes. His eyes tightened, and for the first time she saw the man from the movie in him—the one who crooned No and Yes into his lover's neck.

Power tingled in the room, moved back and forth between them. All those nights ago, with her best friend, she had felt sick watching the movie. Now, she took off her wet clothes, carefully watching his reaction, and then pressed herself against him. He responded weakly, touching her spine with his hand, kissing her shoulders with his mouth. This is my life now, she thought, I have to love my life.

Across the neighborhood, the ladies called one another after dinner to talk about the new woman, about the strange lunch and the goat, some of them holding the phone receivers and standing in their windows, their glances drawn to the new couple's house. She'll learn, they concluded one by one, and then, slightly more wistfully, as if remembering some time from long ago, We'll see. In their bedrooms, the little girls—torturers of goats and fearers of snakes—slept soundly next to glasses of water, night-lights firmly on, dreams wandering up to the moon slung like a jackknife in the bright, starry sky.

A LIST OF PLACES MY MOTHER WAS OLD

1. My mother is old at the yogurt shop. The small storefront tucked in between two pharmacies, the inside walls painted white. A boy ladles yogurt into a polyethylene bag, hair parted to the left with clumps of gel.
2. My mother is old in the car sitting next to me as I drive, my wrists tight and young in front of me, hands on the wheel, wrinkle free.
3. My mother is old at the butcher's, walking through flies buzzing around hanging carcasses, a prophet in the wrong part of town.
4. My mother is old when we have guests over. She watches the kitchen door while the guests talk to one another. She waits for the juice, worried about the arrangements. Have you had enough to eat?
5. My mother is old when she walks like all the women in her family, when I walk like her. She doesn't put one foot after the other; she puts her feet to the side turn by turn, like a bird waddling.
6. My mother used to be beautiful but now she is old. Now she has a chicken face, mouth stretched into a straight flat line, chin drooping, expression befuddled.

7. When my mother becomes old, I see her in sharp focus. She wears her clothes with grace but her hair is white, her face falls under a weight, she walks with a limp. She is not invisible.
8. My mother becomes old after my father falls sick.
9. My mother becomes old when she fearfully talks about love and its ending.
10. My mother becomes old when I tell her about my life plans. I am not in love but I am trying to be, with a boy who lives in another country. Her life rides circles around me.
11. My mother becomes old when she's twenty-two and has her first miscarriage. Afterward my aunt (my father's cousin) looks her up and down and says, Maybe something is wrong with your body. Ten more years until this statement is proved wrong. Even then, it is only proved half wrong because she has twins, one of them dead, one of them me.
12. For two days they let my suddenly old mother believe my twin brother is alive. When I am handed to her alone, she loves me with the love she had reserved for two babies. I'm two in one, she tells me as I grow up.
13. My mother becomes old when, thirty-seven years into their marriage, my father cries. When he says, I have lost all control, weeping exhausted into his plate at the dinner table. She looks at him then and becomes a tree growing out of the chair she is sitting on, taller and taller, ready to engulf him and his fear of dying. I watch her do this for the rest of his life. Two months and three days, to be exact.
14. My mother becomes old when my younger brother tells her he cannot live in the house with her. He says, I have a life. The statement is clean and clear and free of guilt. He is a boy. Sons take care of their mothers, she says in response.

15. My mother becomes old when she has to show me how to be a son. She says I must be kind, I must be compromising. She says I must not worry too much.
16. I am born when my mother is already old. I know her as old even though I have a picture of her on my table in which she is wearing a white shalwar kameez and standing with her sisters on a path leading up to their childhood home. The three of them stare sepia-faced at the camera, the youngest with her thumb in her mouth. My mother has short hair in the picture—something she always objected to when I was growing up—and she is staring, angry, into the lens as if she knows what is coming.
17. My mother will grow old. I am sorry she is old. I want to see us waving and bright, together like birds in the sky. How will we tally what the years took from us? Her children's childhoods, her husband, her own parents, supple limbs and short hair, as seen in pictures. My life in other countries.
18. One day my old mother tells me that as a girl she spent an entire year growing out her hair, oiling it every weekend, carefully wrapping it in coils and tying it up for hours. She says she did all the fashion of the years, the flares and the small, tight shirts. She says she wore makeup on her eyelids, tipped the ends of her liner like the wings of a free parrot. She says she loved my father even though he could be cruel sometimes, as people we love often are. She says they had many years of love. My mother says she is sad my twin died. My mother also says she lived a full life and now I must live mine, though I must stay. My mother says the right thing happens to you, and sometimes the wrong thing happens to you and maybe this is all the wrong thing but you must take it, the good and the bad, and feed on it until you are young again.

THE MAN WHO FLEW

The man squatting in the unfinished house is learning how to fly. Every morning for the past few months, I've seen him scavenging around our neighborhood for discarded pajamas, shirts, bedsheets, linen, and plastic bags. He pokes at things with a large stick, overturns them, and then reaches to pick them up gently, holding them between his thumb and forefinger as if he is one of those people who examines rare, dead birds for a living. He carries the things up to the unfinished house. It is really just a skeleton of a house, no doors, windows, paint. I watch this man closely because our neighbor believes he is a spy. The neighbor's house is next to the unfinished house and ours is opposite both. Why else would he need to collect all that junk? she asks when she comes over to drink tea with my mother. It's a front for all the spying he's doing for our country's intelligence services. The neighbor has to enunciate clearly and come right up to my mother's face to make herself heard. Both women are in their late seventies, almost double my age. Once they must have attracted attention. Now their conversation fritters about in the air. The neighbor thinks our lives deserve to be spied upon. At times, I find myself believing her stories. After all, the man does spy on me, especially when in the middle of the afternoon, I lie back on my bed and masturbate. He sits on the third floor of the unfinished house and stares right at me as the sun shines down on us both. Sometimes he is also naked but he never touches himself while he watches me. His arms stay by his side. He might be a spy but he is an honorable spy.

I have lived in this house my whole life. Lately, I have become immune to stares anyway. I believe people should be able to watch one another in order to increase the chances of understanding themselves. I wonder what the man thinks as he watches me touch myself. Is he aroused or unhappy or does he think I am bold? Maybe he thinks I am the boldest woman on the planet. Always, I take my pants all the way off, I never leave underwear on. I never cover myself with a sheet. I make sure the curtains are wide open. Sometimes if he is not there to watch me, I feel a kind of sorrow. It is a privilege to have a person witness your life.

The man does not own the house he is squatting in. In fact, that house was abandoned because the neighbor put a curse on it. This she also tells my mother during her visits to our house. She says, I just prayed and prayed that that house would never be finished, because can you imagine if someone moved in there? They would be able to see straight into our garden and then our lives would be ruined. The neighbor always talks about herself as if she lives with another person, though her husband died years ago. He died of a heart attack. She also says about this time, I was so scared. God has given her some power though, because her curse works. The house floods when it rains. There is something fundamentally wrong with the foundation, she says with satisfaction. Can you believe God listens to me?

I think this is why I let the man watch me in the afternoons. It seems particularly unfair that God listens to the neighbor but not to me or the man squatting in the unfinished house. After all, he must also have his own desires, living as he is in an unfinished house. When it rains, the man piles his collection of clothes and bedsheets and linen in the corner of the room that slants upward so the rainwater does not get any of his things wet. Me, I would personally like to get a job. I have been unemployed for four years and five days now. I live alone, or as alone as someone can who lives with their mother. By watching him, I think I have become a kinder, more wholesome person.

I know he is learning how to fly because yesterday we spoke for the first time. I was listening to music in my room and noticed from my window that he was swaying by himself, a torch resting in a corner of the room. He was spotlit, as if he were an angel or forsaken or both. I considered this a sign.

What are you doing? I screamed.

Nothing, he replied.

Then, becoming a little bolder, I asked straightaway, Why are you collecting the clothes?

I'm going to fly.

He gestured seriously to all his things. In the dark, and lit up by the flashlight, he did not look as if he harbored any designs. It seemed pure, his desire to fly. As I watched, he held a torn bedsheet to his cheek, tenderly enough to make me want to cry.

Today in the afternoon, the neighbor comes over and speaks to my mother in the kitchen. She says, Your daughter was talking to the squatter last night. She says this with a crooked mouth, as if something bad is parked on her tongue and she can taste it when she speaks. My mother is hard of hearing and has cataracts covering her eyes. The neighbor repeats herself and then the horror is written on my mother's face. Sorry, she tells the neighbor, I'm so sorry, until the neighbor leaves. My mother's best friend in the world is her brother, my uncle who is twenty years younger than her. That night my mother locks herself in her room and says to him on the phone, I just can't believe she has no honor.

Everyone says women in this country are repressed. What came first, the mother or the repression? I cannot get married because who will look after my mother if I do? Anyway, I don't want to get married. Why would I exchange a house for another house? Brick is the same everywhere. When the unfinished house is finished it will be the same as our house. The people living in it will be the same as us. I am growing old in this house with my mother. I am thirty-four. According to the Internet these are my prime sexual years.

My uncle comes right over. He screams for a long time. I say, Jee, jee, jee at every turn. My uncle is a very effective yeller. I am scared of him. But still, that night after he leaves, I open my window and yell, The neighbor is a slut! I see her old bitch face looking out of her window. The man in the unfinished house cheers and joins me in the chant, The neighbor is a slut! The neighbor is a slut!

Finally, when my voice is about to disappear, I ask him, How are you today?

Good, my sister, he answers. He holds up a bedsheet and ties it to another.

Are all the bedsheets from the trash?

I steal some from houses at night, he says. You would be surprised at what people don't notice has gone missing.

Have you stolen any from us?

You? Never!

How will you fly?

He grins at me and says, You have to come see.

I say nothing then, because we both hear the neighbor unlatching and latching her gate. She is wearing small, black wedge heels, her hair shines. Her cheeks glow red. She comes all the way to our house again, rings and rings the bell. Finally, I open the door. It is nighttime now. She was just here in the afternoon. Spring is blooming into summer. Mosquitoes buzz above her head, ready to feed on her. I should leave her out there, she is frothing at the mouth. How dare you? she says. Finally, my mother, who fell asleep after my uncle left, wakes. She's terrified to see the neighbor again, twice in one day! My mother hates confrontation, hates people who face a thing directly.

Your daughter called me a slut, the neighbor yells at my mother and my mother looks shocked. She looks at me uncertainly and it breaks my heart that I have had to watch her get this old. Children should leave their parents at some point or they erupt at the most inopportune moments, turning everything around them into ash. I'm sorry, I whisper. Suddenly, I feel like crying. I'm sorry, I tell the aunty. From the other house, the squatter's voice carries. Boo, he says. Boo! He does not like that I am apologizing. I understand why. He and I are the same, you see. We both have nowhere else to go and people with nowhere to go have to stand their ground or they lose it very quickly.

The neighbor tells my mother, She's a curse on your house and if she were my daughter, I would have disowned her by now. If I was beautiful, I wonder if she would be gentler with me. I start to cry and say, I'm sorry, I just don't know what to do with myself. Get a job! The neighbor yells and then she walks off in a huff. My mother looks at me. You are a curse, she says. In my old age, I just want peace. I can give you that, I plead with her. That's the purpose of my life. If I am failing at even that, what is the point? She comes forward and holds both my hands gently then. She is very tired. She is aged, aging, gone. Where are the tomes written about the heartbreak of watching your parents disappear before your very eyes?

I love you, she says. And the neighbor is too old to be a slut. Moths circle our heads before crackling into the light bulb lighting up the porch. Sometimes my mother is like a plant I have just watered, thrusting—refreshed—up in the air.

The squatter in the house opposite ours is learning to fly, I tell my mother. She shrugs. Your uncle was right, she says. We have to be careful of these men, and then the light in her eyes goes dim again and she shuffles back to her room.

Soon her snores fill up the house, I turn off all the lights and slowly tiptoe outside, latch and unlatch the gate and take care to walk on the side of the road that is away from the light of the streetlamps. I make my way to the bramble surrounding the unfinished house and push it out of the way with my arms. The scratches begin to bleed, the blood invites mosquitoes. They rest on my arms like guards as I enter the house. I climb the stairs to the third floor where the squatter is sitting. He beams.

You're here!

Show me how to fly, I tell him.

He looks at me seriously. Okay, he says. But if you're trying to kill yourself, this is not the way to do it.

I take a moment to consider. I am not trying to kill myself, I finally say, but if I die in the process of trying to fly, I won't mind.

Okay, he says. Good answer.

He holds up a bedsheet. It's patterned with tulips and leaves, long stems. That's beautiful, I tell him.

It's from a rich man's house, he replies.

There is no moon tonight. Mountains, trees, shrubs, bushes—everything coalesces into one dark mass. Only one light shines on, in the neighbor's bedroom window. He sees me eyeing it. She's not a nice lady, he says. I nod.

He hands me the sheet and finds another one for himself. On both, he's stitched yellow netting on the top and bottom so the sheet feels sturdier. He's cut and sewn the ends together so they are narrow. I hold what looks like one gigantic bonnet. He holds another. We both walk to the edge of the room, toward the shape of a window that was never finished. His things lie around us on the floor everywhere.

Have you ever done this before? I ask him.

No.

We both stand on the ledge. We hold the sheets in our hands and stare down at the buzzing ground. The air at night is cooler.

Why don't you touch yourself when I am touching myself in the afternoons?

I don't realize the question has been bothering me until I ask it.

You are like my sister, he says. I feel like I know you.

Thank you, I say. This could be our last night on the planet.

It won't be, he says, confidently.

I touch his arm and he touches mine, just in case this is the last time we get to feel someone alive next to us. A bird has made a nest in his room. Three little babies mewl away. The world is as beautiful as we want it to be.

Are you a spy? I ask him.

No, he says. I'm homeless.

Okay, enough distractions, he adds. Let's go. We both look at the birds. Maybe I won't get to see this summer. This time of year is the most beautiful time of the year. My mother has the gardener plant zinnias and azaleas and tulips in our small front yard. New grass grows clean and sharp out of the ground. The sunsets break everyone's hearts. You can hear everyone living in the city, like go go go! And yet, I am always at the edge of it.

Okay, the squatter says, on three.

One.

Two.

Three.

He walks off the ledge first and I close my eyes and follow, holding the sheet's ends in my hands. The net is stiff, digs into my palms. For a second, I think, What have I done? The sheet's body is flat first, and then suddenly it balloons above me and I slow a little and my heart shudders in relief. You go slower if you cycle with your legs, he yells just as he lands. Maybe it takes two seconds before my feet push into the shrubbery on the ground, hard. I stumble a little, and then stand. My eyes are used to the dark now, and I see he is breathing hard and weeping. Then the bedsheet lands on me and he disappears.

I did it, he says. I finally did something.

I am surprised that my face is wet too. You did, I say. I want to offer more, but I realize with a small shard of joy that I don't want to offer myself. This is the thing, you use who you can and then you move onward and it is a blessing there is an onward to walk toward. I should have had sex with you, he says, aware that this is where we part ways. He skips back toward the mouth of the house. We can fly! His teeth shine in the night. I watch him disappear.

That night, when I go home, I change out of my dusty clothes and close my curtains for the first time in a long time, listening to my heart thump from the shock of being reminded that it is alive. Tomorrow, I promise, I will go to my neighbor's house and apologize. I will cook a meal for my mother and massage her legs. I will sit with her while she eats it and talk about mundane things. I will smile when she smiles even though she can barely see me, and later, I will take out the trash and haggle over the price of water with the Nestlé people who come weekly to deliver the large plastic bottles of water. Through the slow slog of the years ahead this cool, joyous night will glide beside me like a shadow and a prayer. I promise I will be fine passing my time minute by minute, hour by hour like everyone else in this country.

NAJWA

Najwa baji was my favorite cousin. When I was younger I visited her house often. The two of us would go up to her bedroom where she paced the carpet, sometimes taking a break to touch one of the dolls arranged on her bedside table. We were competitive about our dolls. When I was visiting she always made a show of inspecting them carefully, one ear turned toward me to show she was listening.

On these long afternoons, I sat on her bed and talked endlessly: I didn't like drinking milk at night, the other girls at school were boring, I hadn't found any real friends even though in all the books I'd read girls my age always had best friends. I'd heave a sigh when I was done and then she would say, And? Najwa baji was always looking for the ends of things even after I thought I'd found them. And nothing, I'd reply. She knew I was impatient with the question but still she pressed me until I gave her more. When some time had passed and I had exhausted myself we would both go down to the TV lounge, a corner of which was taken up by the treadmill my uncle had bought years ago. Sometimes she would jump on its belt and start running. Her frock flew up behind her, exposing her underwear, which was of the type old women wear, almost like shorts, brightly colored but laced near the bottom and clinging to her thighs. I always felt ashamed as she ran, panting harder and harder, her thumb pressing the speed button. Can you do this? she would yell over the sound of the machine; I always shook my head, dutiful as younger cousins are meant to be.

When we became teenagers she pierced the cartilage in her ear in three different places very close to one another. She went after school with a friend.

She had told her father she was visiting me, and I—like an idiot—denied knowing anything when he called. I looked out at the street from my bedroom window, the phone receiver pressed to my ear. Later, Najwa baji told me he beat her with his hardest leather shoe and made her take out the piercings. Good, I said, feeling righteous, what were you thinking?

We were always losing things at Najwa baji's house because my uncle was always putting them away. Even my mother said he could use some help and he was her favorite out of her three brothers. He could not pass a bed without folding down the sheet's corners, could not pass a table without dusting the surface with a hand. He often said when I went over that cleanliness was God's way. That a clean person was the closest to heaven. However hard we tried, Najwa baji and I could not find his zeal inside ourselves.

We went to the same school but she was two classes above me. We never talked during lunch break and when she passed me by she would deliberately turn her head. Once I overheard one of her friends asking her if I was her cousin. Yeah, she said, casually. And that was it. There was the time when I was in sixth grade and the senior girls were practicing throwing javelins over the sand pit near the swing set. Whenever it was her turn the girls would line up on either side of the pit. Najwa baji would hoist her shalwar higher and grit her whole face in concentration before arching her arm. The girls always cheered hardest for her. Even though not many people knew I was her cousin I still felt it was a card I could play. It was something I kept close to myself at school and it comforted me when I was having a particularly bad day.

We came together at home time when my uncle drove us both back. I lived close to her in a house painted with a yellow border. Sometimes it took us longer to get home because my uncle needed to drive exactly in the middle lane.

When we got to my house my uncle always accepted my mother's offering of juice. Najwa baji also accepted, trailing her school bag into the house with a weariness that indicated she had come to stay. My mother did not like her very much. My uncle picked up the things around the kitchen and put them away; my mother had long since stopped telling him it was her house. He can't help himself, she told me once. It was the first time it had occurred to me that something could be out of a person's control. I had always felt if I stuck close to the rules and listened like my mother told me to I would be fine. Perhaps this is where Najwa baji got her courage from. She must have known too about things being out of people's control, about how whether or not you want to be a certain way, you sometimes just were. Which is why, at eighteen, she fell in love.

It was her last year at school and I was starting to miss her already. She still came over but now she was less competitive. I missed her taking an interest in my life. At school she sat huddled with her friends near the small bunch of trees that formed a makeshift hut. Where would she meet a boy? We went straight home from school together and then spent the day under the watchful eyes of our parents. Her family wasn't very rich and lived in a small two-bedroom apartment over three small storefronts. Their biggest luxury was the treadmill. If I went over in the evenings, Najwa baji and I would walk up and down the terrace of the building. Our parents had told us when we were growing up that we were not allowed to go near the edges of the roof so the shopkeepers wouldn't be tempted to look up at us. We were always careful to stay in the middle, keeping our voices low. We stopped walking up there after she started to love this boy.

My uncle called me one evening around 8:00 p.m. on a school night and asked me if I knew where she was. I remembered the ear cartilage from all those years ago and said, Yes, she's with me. He asked me to put her on the phone and I tried to stall. She's in the toilet, I said. He told me to get my mother. My mother took the receiver from me first wiping her hands on a small towel she was holding. I saw her face puzzle over, the lines near her temples creasing softly and then unfurling in understanding.

It's a mark of how well my mother knew me that she didn't ask, as she twisted my earlobe between her thumb and forefinger, where my cousin was. Instead she asked, Why did you lie? Why? she asked again, bending my head forward and smacking me against the ear. I said sorry immediately of course and told her I didn't know where she was. I understood I would get in trouble if it turned out I was keeping Najwa baji's secret. Everybody knew everybody else in the neighborhood and reputations depended on who did what and with whom. Let's go, my mother said, grabbing her dupatta and calling out to my father who was in the TV lounge. We'll be back, she said.

We walked the short distance to my uncle's house, me trying to keep up with my mother's hurried steps as she muttered under her breath. Daughters, she said, where do you keep them? The sun was setting and the sky was a soft-hued orange and blue. When we got to my uncle's apartment building, we noticed that the door had been propped open with a brick. Potted bougainvilleas lined either side of the doorway. My aunt had been trying to get them to grow a little so she could arrange them on top of the terrace. She was a beautiful woman, my aunt, and often people told us that Najwa baji took after her.

My uncle was sitting on the floor of the living room on a cushion, his eyes were trained on his hands. He was holding a tissue which he folded into halves and then tore, exactly in the middle, before folding that over and doing it again. The living room floor was covered in small squares of white. My aunt leaned over him saying, She's fine. He didn't even look up when my mother touched his shoulder. He just shook his head. We went through Najwa's phone, my aunt said in a low voice, looking first at me, did you know? I shook my head, wondered what they had found. It was a big thing, to be in love. Surely, I thought, if that is what had happened to her, my uncle would understand.

My mother had always said my uncle had loved my aunt since he was a little boy. He had followed her to school when he was five years old, every day until her parents complained. My mother always laughed when she told the story. She said it was obvious my aunt's parents felt very silly when they came to complain about the small five-year-old boy. They could not keep from smiling but still it unsettled them, his love for their daughter.

The story was that my aunt was never oblivious of his love but she remained wary of the boy who folded his glasses just so after he was done reading, who stepped only on the right squares when he was walking in the quad. She said yes to marrying him because she felt she had to give someone a chance who was so particular about everything. Isn't it wonderful, she always said to everyone, that such a particular man is particular about us? I wonder how Najwa baji felt when she heard this excuse.

We sat with my uncle for two hours. Outside, the sun went down and the streetlights came on. My aunt, trying to be hospitable, talked for a little bit but eventually gave up. My mother went into the kitchen to see if she could make something to eat. I did not know if we were angry or worried or both and tried to instill all of these feelings in myself. I knew without a doubt that Najwa baji would come because she loved her parents. Especially her father. I had once tried making fun of my uncle by walking in the house like a robot, picking up and moving away all the objects in my path. She had watched me for a second before flying at me, a tall girl in a bright blue-red frock, scoop necked so her collarbones popped. When I finally managed to pull myself away, crying and bleeding, I noticed that her face was wet. I never said a word about it again, especially to her.

We waited for another hour before we heard the door at the bottom creak open. My uncle's hands stilled and my aunt also became very quiet. When Najwa baji walked in she looked the same as always, glowing and light. A thin sheen of sweat at the top of her forehead. It's so hot outside, she was saying, not really looking at any of us. She didn't notice anything was wrong. This struck me as the strangest thing. That she had no idea that her world was being redrawn by her parents.

Where were you? Even then, it was my mother who spoke. I wanted to beg her to shut up. Sometimes I felt my family—my mother, my father, and I—should move far, far away. When something happened it showed in my mother's face, clear as lines. When I was older, I promised myself, I would detach myself from everything and re-form new, tenuous bonds with normal people, people who did not sit in your throat all day long.

I was at school, Najwa baji said, her voice still light and tired. Perhaps, I thought, everyone was wrong.

I'm sorry I left my phone at home. She looked up and noticed everyone's faces. My uncle had run out of tissue and was simply turning his hands. The shopkeepers downstairs had the television blaring and we could hear their laughter lift in the air and settle in the stifling room.

When we were children we had crouched in the lawn together, Najwa baji and I, our faces to the grass looking for the small red bodies of ladybugs. We had spent entire afternoons watching them crawl across our hands, moaning whenever they took off in flight. This was the image that came in my head when I thought about her impending death. My uncle would kill her. I saw him take the phone from my aunt's hands and I looked away in case what happened next replaced those summer afternoons, knee-stained and dizzy from the heat.

By now Najwa baji was standing very still. She was wearing a red shirt, two maroon half-moons staining the place under her armpits; she looked disjointed in the light coming in from the window. Abba, she said. I wanted her to be quiet, to not disturb anything. My uncle had big hands, hairy around the knuckles.

Somewhere deep down, I was wondering why my mother hadn't sent me away yet. Maybe she wanted me to see what happened to women who strayed, to witness penance. I was startled by the anger inside me, by the thought that suddenly appeared as I looked at my frightened cousin, now looking younger than her eighteen years. This is what you get, I thought.

I saw the shadow of my uncle lengthen as he stood. My mother put herself between him and his daughter. Rehan, she said, we should ask her what happened, at which Najwa baji made a sound of relief. I stared at Najwa baji's ears. Even in the dark, I imagined I could see three small raised bumps in the left ear, closed over long ago.

Let me read some of these, began my uncle, holding her phone. His voice was suddenly very light. He spoke as if he was talking to a friend. My cousin shrank into the door through which she'd just entered, now closed. Abba, it's not—

He began to murmur, Let me see, let me see. This is where it begins. Hello, I saw you walking today. You're so beautiful. My uncle laughed after this. Isn't it funny, he said. That that's all it takes these days?

Nobody replied and my cousin looked at her feet, only looking up when my uncle spoke again, There's a reply. He switched his voice to a high girlish giggle. Who is this? Is this Asad?

Yes, my name is Asad. Do you want to know anything else?

No.

Where did you get this number?

I asked the guard to find it from the school records.

Why?

How did you know this was Asad?

My uncle began to enjoy himself. He used a deep baritone voice for the boy (I could not bear to think of him by name) and switched to a high shriek for Najwa baji. He became bolder as he read, and when I finally dared to look at him, I saw he had turned into a carefree man I didn't recognize. He touched his chest when a message mentioned the heart, his lips when either of them mentioned kissing. He took up the whole living room as he acted out their messages, expanding his performance as Najwa baji's responses went from curt to accepting to loving, taking his eyes off the phone occasionally to glance over at my cousin. My uncle faced Najwa baji's terror, coaxing it to grow bigger. The pieces of tissue fluttered around his feet.

Love you, good night, the boy's last message said, to which Najwa baji had replied, I love you too. My uncle sang the last part, mimicking his daughter, puckering his lips at her and then beginning to clap.

Well, he said, what do you think? Should we take this downstairs? It was very sweet. I think the shopkeepers would like to hear this too, don't you? I decided I hated him when he started to walk to the back bedroom windows. Hey, I could hear him yelling, do you gentlemen want to hear a love story? A cheer went up in the shops. I looked at my aunt and my mother. I could hear Najwa baji crying. I hate it, she was saying, I hate it here.

Then you can leave. He spoke quietly but the apartment was small and his voice carried. I could see their silhouettes in the other room. He was holding the phone out to Najwa baji. Call him, he said, and tell him to come. My cousin didn't move but after a second or two had passed she began to dial.

She said Hello and then paused as he said something in return. Then, They found out. The last bit a sob. The boy said something and Najwa baji looked at my uncle, who did not speak or even look at her. Can you come?

The boy said something on the other line and Najwa baji did not say anything back. When she hung up, my uncle asked, Is he coming? I think she nodded. Good, he said, then pack your things.

I started to cry finally. My mother folded me in her arms as if to say it would not happen to me but I knew that it would not happen to me because of the way I carried myself in the world and not because she would defend me. I felt her warm body and wondered what was necessary and what was not.

Najwa baji packed. During that time my aunt and uncle did not go near her. Finally, she had a small bag. She looked grown up, the tears had made her face swell. I stared at her and hoped this was what she wanted and what was good for her.

After she left, I went to the window overlooking the street and saw her standing by the roadside downstairs. My aunt and my uncle went to bed but my mother and I stayed in the apartment for a long time.

The boy never came. When we went downstairs to walk back home she was still standing by the side of the road, her blue duffel bag resting beside her. My mother made a small, strangled noise in her throat. I thought of that girl all those years ago, running on the treadmill, teeth misaligned and panting as she ran, Can you do this?

My mother walked straight up to Najwa baji and folded a hand down the length of her hair. She did not bend to my mother but my mother pulled her in anyway and said, Come home with us. The worst of it, I thought, was over. We walked her back to our house.

My mother made her voice cheerful for our father when we entered. Smile, she hissed at us, or your father will know. Najwa baji and I smiled at my father, who was sitting in front of the television. Najwa's sleeping over, my mother said to my father, who nodded at the television screen.

Najwa baji walked behind me to my room. She didn't unpack her duffel bag, or take out any of her clothes and instead only slipped off her shoes and slipped into bed like someone moving underwater. She shut her eyes immediately. I moved around a little at first, to change and to brush my teeth but soon turned off the light and got into bed.

She lay with her back pressed against mine so I could feel the heat coming off her. I wanted to tell her I did not hate her and that I was sorry but the words stayed still and deep inside some part of me that could not be pried open.

At some point, I woke up in the night and saw that she had unfurled like a small glowing starfish. Her face shone, loose in sleep. Tomorrow, I knew, or the day after, my mother would take her back home. My uncle would forgive her in a few weeks, maybe a month. I wondered where her life would go from there. There's no rest, my father sometimes said, for sinners. But she looked peaceful as she slept.

I hoped she would fall in love again and that I would fall in love even once. At the time I did not know any boys, did not know where I would meet any, though I was beginning to notice them standing outside my school during home time, gawkish and watchful as the girls entered and exited. Maybe this is how she had met him. I was overtaken by compassion as I lay there thinking of a boy approaching me outside school and me not wanting to but starting to like him despite myself. This seemed incredibly romantic. I wanted Najwa baji and I to be like sisters and one day I hoped we would laugh about tonight. I would ask her what had annoyed her more, her father or the boy never coming and she'd giggle and lean in and say, Both of course! Men! Loosely waving the word around like a small handkerchief.

But first we had the morning to contend with, and then the next morning and then the next before we could pretend to forget about this, like we had forgotten about the ear piercings. It occurred to me that this is why she had always asked me to go on with my stories, teasing out as much as she could before finally giving up. Perhaps she knew there would always be more after the last, awful part.

THE PARK

We rejoice when the government names the park after the country's mother—Fatima Jinnah Park—and sets it in the middle of the capital city. A whole park named after the Madar-e-Millat, my mother says with a squint, staring at the newspaper article under the apple tree in Naila aunty's garden. Let's move here, she says, chewing on one of the apples. I am seventeen. We two churails have lived in this garden for seven years because of me.

My mother starts a routine of waking in the morning and flipping through the newspaper pages. I don't know what she's looking for but daily she announces, It isn't time yet. Then I spend the rest of the day as I normally do, staring at Naila aunty as she potters around the garden, as she reads, as she sometimes comes outside with her bright-red gardening can to water the plants in the heat of this June. Sometimes her son, Rayyab, comes to visit her, but he hasn't visited in months. Naila aunty's husband left her a long time ago. Every day her life shows me that the ways marriage can mark a person are endless, but sometimes it can all still equal to nothing.

A month passes and July arrives. The garden crackles with heat and the air around us is hazy with dust. I lie in the garden next to my mother on a Friday, and we use the newspaper to fan ourselves. This morning, my mother has read that small sculptures have popped up around the park: domed structures, bridges wrapped in green trellis, rock gardens and small ponds all designed some space apart from one another by the country's famous architects. We'll go tomorrow, she says as we lie there, and I know that our time in the garden is over.

During that last night I weep on the grass, grief struck but electric with anticipation. Naila aunty comes to stand at her window for a second before drawing the curtain closed. My mother holds me and says, It's time now, she doesn't need us anymore. When the morning arrives, we gather our things. There isn't much we have with us. One suitcase, in which I pack some of my books, and all our shalwar kameezes.

We enter the park through the main gate, straight into the heart of the late, green afternoon. The grass near where we are is freshly cut. In the distance, men in orange vests whir tractors across patches of green that still need trimming. The main pathway leads to a children's playground, the only section of the park surrounded by a wire mesh fence. Within the fenced area are gleaming swings, slides, seesaws, ten merry-go-rounds on which little girls and boys are soaring in circles. As we walk, my mother and I notice bushes and knotted trees under which lovers stare at each other, waiting for the chance to touch without being seen. Families take up larger patches of grass and play cricket. Two young women set up a badminton net and begin to swing their arms, following the wide arc of the shuttlecock with their bodies.

The world exists for exactly this feeling, my mother says, her eyes shining with hope.

We visit all the domed structures in the park one by one. Finally, we find it. My mother, who knows things before they happen, grows tall and lovely as she stands staring at our new home. We pause at the entrance, say a little prayer, and then step inside. On some days I am sad about the limits of my life but on others, like this one, I am buoyed by the fact that I am destined to be my mother and the world lies open and free at my feet.

The entrance to the domed structure points straight to a pulpit nestled between two curved staircases. The stairs lead down to a small concrete stage.

Maybe this is supposed to be a theater, I say.

My mother agrees, Oh, this will be excellent for the work we do.

Four columns wrought of colorful stone—two on either side of the curved stage—hold up the dome. The light from the sun enters the space and bounces off the stonework, causing the whole place to glow. We will be happy here, my mother finally says, and I think of Naila aunty, home alone now, and nod.

As the sun descends and twilight spreads across the sky shade by shade, we make ourselves comfortable. Outside, we can hear families starting to depart. You never know what lurks in wide-open spaces or under trees in the dark. Some say the park is built on a graveyard, but tonight my mother scoffs at this. All places are built on the backs of someone else's death, she says. Outside, women are probably telling their children they have to get home before the churails start wandering under the trees, the *chur* in the name reminding little girls and boys clinging to their parents of rats sucking on skin, the *ail*, of a long, unending wail.

As I drift off, I hear my mother whisper, We begin tomorrow. I think about how in this place too, I will love her as I have always loved her, aware that the lack of her love could kill me, driven always by fear of its ending. That night the two of us sleep right in the middle of the stage, mosquitoes chewing lightly on our bodies.

Sunday is the day I am supposed to finally turn into my mother. In the morning, she watches me closely as I dress, nods approvingly when I hold up the shalwar kameez with the round neck, the one that shows off my collarbone as if it is a necklace someone can take off my body. I leave my hair long down my back and slip on sandals with gems pasted on the straps. My feet glitter. As usual, my mother looks beautiful and fresh, as if she woke up having already feasted in the night on the blood of those who have done wrong in the world. We make our way to the main entrance. She pats me on the back as she walks.

This is God's work, she says. This is what you were always meant to do. We've delayed it too long already.

We stand under a large tree between the children's playground and the main entrance, watching people begin to trickle in. I wonder what Naila aunty is doing. By now she must be awake and showered, the smell of shampoo and conditioner wafting in the room as she brushes the tangles out of her wet hair.

You can spot a certain kind of man—the kind we are looking for—in a crowd of a thousand people. We see him the moment he enters the park. He's in a starched lime-green shalwar kameez, the vest visible through his clothes, and his wife and little girl are on either side of him. The girl cannot be older than seven or eight. My heart twists, remembers Naila aunty's son, Rayyab, and then I put his face out of my mind. He is a grown man by now.

My mother's eyes brighten as she stares at the family. The woman is holding a piece of tissue paper and twisting it between her fingers. It is red from the lipstick she has wiped off. As she wrings the tissue in her hands, small strands break off and fly onto the concrete. One of them comes to rest near our feet. The smell of fear is so strong by now that I begin to get heady with it. My mother licks her lips.

When they get to the gate of the children's playground, the man pays the thirty Rs. ticket price and bends to look into his daughter's face. He smiles at her gently and motions for her to go in. We strain our ears to hear. We'll be in in a second, he says. The girl glances between her parents' faces and her mother gives her a watery smile. She disappears into the park and soon we can see her red frock standing by a small merry-go-round.

Now my mother and I focus on drowning out the noise in the park and one by one the sounds of the other children, of men selling pappar, of families chattering fall away. All we hear are the man and the woman. He leads her to a corner. He says, his mouth hard, his face starched stiff as his clothes, Why are you always embarrassing me?

Little birds, robins, begin to line the main walkway. She brings what remains of the tissue to her lips, rubs them quickly. His kameez blows up in the breeze.

I thought you would like it, she says. It was a present from Rubina. And then she adds, tremulous, just beginning to shake, Why didn't you say anything before we left the house?

I wanted to see if you knew what was good from bad, he says, and Rubina is a slut.

A pause, then, Are you a slut?

When she shakes her head, it seems to make him angrier. He lifts his hand and a few people glance at them. Their little girl is on the merry-go-round now. She is a spinning red top in the background.

My mother sang me a lullaby when I was younger, something I think she made up, *No one knows what they are doing until they have done it*, leaning close to my face and making her voice deep at the end so I would shriek with laughter. She hums the tune now and it carries, lilting in the wind.

Nobody stops when the man slaps the woman, once and hard on her face. They have the look of two people who are always in the middle of behaving like this with each other. The robins come closer to my mother and me, as if asking us to intervene. I let the rage course through me, and smile once, beatific, at my mother, who nods, giving me her blessing.

This is not the first time I have set out to become my mother. Suddenly, I am ten again and staring at Naila aunty's house from across the street. Before we had set off for Naila aunty's house that day, my mother had leaned down and looked me straight in the face to say, Someone has to define what is good for you. Why can't it be your mother? This is the way of our life, she continued, everyone has a way of life.

So this is the way of my life now: I watch as the man makes a motion with his hand, asking his wife to go back into the children's playground. She looks nothing like Naila aunty, who was thin and proud all those years ago, with a BA in psychology. From all those nights we watched her, my mother and I became familiar with the sound of her heart ticking. After Mansoor uncle was done with her, she always went first into fourteen-year-old Rayyab's room and put her cheek to the top of his sleeping head, as if she was trying to glean what sort of man he would become. Should all boys be given the chance to grow into men? my mother asked me some nights after the sound of knuckles hitting against flesh had subsided. The question burned itself into my brain. Afterward, when both wife and son had gone to bed, the edges of their terror-struck minds softening into sleep, Mansoor uncle left to see his sisters. We followed to watch him shine through these other houses' windows. Nightly, the sisters welcomed him like a king, said, Mansoor, Mansoor, Mansoor, and one by one he blessed them by paying them attention, and my mother said, Look, they have been taught to believe they are each worth one of his pinkies and I laughed as I was supposed to.

When I reach the man in the starched shalwar kameez, he is smoking near some tall bushes. His eyes widen as I approach. I know I look beautiful. My mother often says, All women have the right to beauty. I hold this thought in my mind now, the twin sister of courage.

When I reach him I say, I love how carefully your clothes are starched.

He's startled, I can tell. They almost always are. He has just taken a puff of his cigarette, and he waits for a second before expelling the smoke from inside his mouth, turning a little away as he does so. He has a short beard, trimmed close to his face, and sweat lining his sideburns and forehead. Thank you, he says.

I lean in and whisper, I think your wife deserved it.

When he smiles at me, I feel what it would be like to love him, terrible but also all-consuming, no room for your own thoughts.

He comes to stand next to me, pivoting so he is facing the bushes, and nudges me to pivot too. We hear a thud somewhere in the back, a child begins to cry. His arm brushes against mine. My mother's eyes bore a congratulations into my back. Her relief is audible. I know she has thought that because of what happened all those years ago, I may never be able to come into my own.

He says, You don't seem like someone who would wear lipstick if your husband didn't want you to.

I say, I never wear anything I'm not supposed to be wearing.

I widen my eyes a little when I speak, and I can see that he is excited, that he thinks I am one of those women who sleep with men and ask for nothing later, maybe some money. His hand finds the small of my back.

I say, I know a place.

He grows still when he hears this, glances back at the playground. My eyes feel blurry and over focused. My mother's song carries over from my childhood into the middle of this hour and minute, Nobody knows what they're doing until they've done it. Okay he says, and I run a finger up and down his forearm. His breath catches a little. In my mother's voice I say, I'd like to examine these clothes more closely, holding the end of his kameez between my fingers.

Okay, he breathes again, growing very still, excitement coming off him in waves.

Do you mind, I make my voice very soft, if my mother comes too?

Then he is confused, but before he can think more about it, I point toward her standing a ways behind us. She waves. Oh, she has taken over the park with her beauty, his breath catches, again. Dazed, he repeats himself, Okay.

Sometimes the men do not agree and my mother and I have to try other ways. A rat passes across the walkway. My mother gives a small scream and sways a little. He starts to walk faster toward her. I'm sorry, she says when we reach her and she brings up a hand to wipe her forehead.

Please, he says, they should do something about the rats here.

He is truly under our spell by then. He holds both of our arms in a way that makes it seem like this is the natural progression of things.

His wife comes out of the park, and she stares at him, the pink of her mouth round as a siren on her face, Oh. He doesn't even glance at her. We direct his footsteps toward our new home.

We watched Naila aunty's house for two weeks before we finally entered it. Me at ten, young and pigtailed, my mother glorious beside me. We picked our moment. Naila aunty was upstairs in her room and Mansoor uncle was in his study, headphones in his ears blasting music. Only Rayyab was in the kitchen when we walked through it, and he looked up once but did not see us at all. However many times I play it back in my head now, I cannot un-remember the truest fact of what happened that day: I became overcome with a need for this boy to see me and my mother, to understand what was going to happen, and why.

In the mornings, my mother and I roamed the streets, invisible and on the hunt, and people barely turned toward us. All heroes toil in invisibility, my mother said. But something in me from all those nights of listening to Naila aunty plead with Mansoor uncle was rising to the surface. I thought, Knowing is the only path to change. In Rayyab's way of standing in the kitchen, his posture, the upward curve of his chin, I saw Mansoor uncle. My mother said, Wait here, and she headed toward the study, where Mansoor uncle stood as if by some invisible command as she approached. Rayyab swept his finger across the bottom of a bowl that had some chips in it. He looked upset, moody, as if he was in the middle of some great, private tragedy. I thought of my mother's wrath and suddenly it became clear to me that we would be back one day for Rayyab too, this same circle repeating itself, son after father, me after my mother.

I closed my eyes and concentrated. Rayyab went rigid and walked over to the electrical socket. The kettle was unplugged. I stretched open his ear canal with my mind, and in an instant his head became full of the sound of his father begging my mother for mercy. He tried to open his mouth and could not, and then the fourteen-year-old was kneeling by the socket, he was flipping the switch on, he was putting his fingers on it, all while looking wildly around the room and then, finally, he was pressing into it until he felt a spark, and then another. My mother heard his scream of course, even in the midst of meting out punishment, and she was by my side in seconds, leaving the business with Mansoor uncle unfinished. This was probably the first time she left something halfway done.

———

When we reach the dome my mother nods at me. The man's name is Naser, he has told us on the walk over. He has become bolder by the minute, both his arms are wrapped around our waists as we walk, all of us stepping lightly and happily, together and forward. He is capable of being light and happy of course. We can see this when we walk with him. He caresses us gently and we let him. This is where we were coming? he asks a little uncertainly when we get to the dome.

Yes, I nod and then smile.

He looks dubious about the open space. He is caressing himself too, slowly, his hand dipping occasionally into his shalwar. His eyes have taken on this glazed quality. I do not feel guilty when he follows me straight up to the pulpit. I stand before him and he looks down at the stage from over my shoulder, bringing me close as he does.

Nice, he says lightly.

I make sure he is looking down when it happens. I twist them with my mind. I haven't tried this for years, but my feet crack as they turn in on themselves, turn all the wrong way around so they are facing backwards, the gems on my sandals still glittering. A glow courses through my shoulders, my wrists, my legs. Naser's face fills with horror and that makes me happy—to be seen for what I really am—and he tries to turn, but my mother is behind him. Her feet too have turned.

Follow me, I say. And now my voice booms through the dome. I smile throughout, the way I have seen my mother do it. I think about the girl in the red frock. Is a hunger for calm growing inside her? I wonder if she will miss this man if he disappears.

That day, when my mother saw me standing over Rayyab's twitching body, she shrieked, What are you doing? And then she descended on me so I had to let go of Rayyab's mind. He let out a small, slow whine, almost identical to the one his father was letting out in the other room, and momentarily I felt proud that I possessed my mother's strength, but then we heard steps coming down—Naila aunty—and my mother looked at me and said, This is not how it is supposed to be. I wanted to kill her then. Our life, mine and hers, was supposed to be the same. Still, Naila aunty clomped down the stairs. I began to cry, and my mother stepped next to me, looking between the man and son, for once at a loss for what to do.

Naser follows me down the stairs. His legs twitch as if they are trying to listen to the rest of his body, which is demanding that he run. He whimpers as he walks, his lips sealed shut. My hair braids itself as I lead, coils into three strands and then twists over and over again by itself, the gentleness of this act making me feel calmer until we arrive, the two of us, to stand in the middle of the stage. I look once at my mother, who has followed us down. To him, I say, Do you like lipstick?

He shakes his head no, and pleased with this response, I lean in close, croon, Neither do I. I look him straight in the face and my lips get lighter and lighter until they are the same color as my skin, until you cannot even tell I have lips unless I smile, my teeth sharp and white as a surprise when I open my mouth.

I can see his shalwar is wet now, a slow spreading stain near his crotch.

I just really think, I say, that *everyone* should give *everything* a shot.

Next to me, my mother holds up a small tube of lipstick. She leans in, says, A gift from Rubina.

The thing is, I say, running my hand up and down his arm again, the thing is, I have never learned how to put lipstick on. Would you mind putting it on me?

My mother uncaps the tube for us. Holds it up to his face. Jerkily, his arm rises against his will to take the tube. He whimpers, pleading with his eyes for us to stop.

I think he'd love to put it on you, my mother says to me, making her voice high and girlish.

He brings his hand to my face and slowly starts to color in my lips. He is damp with fear, sweat pooling under his armpits. The smell of urine wafts in the air. I think of the little girl and her anxious glances. I wonder briefly if the mother was to blame. If it should be her we have in here.

Why do we do this? My mother says it is our duty.

I tell my mother, Tell me if he goes outside my lip line okay? She nods, going very still. I can tell that she is proud of me, that I have exceeded her expectations today. But she should not have worried. How long can a person remain ashamed of their one true nature?

Oh, he just went outside your lip line, my mother says sympathetically.

And then I let it enter me, the hatred I had felt that day when I saw Rayyab leaning against the counter. I raise my arm and bring it down against Naser's face so hard that there is a sound like cracking in the air. His bottom lip begins to bleed.

But he cannot stop of course, he continues to paint my face as tears spurt from his eyes, and my mother says, Oh he's missed a spot, oh he missed again! over and over again and each time she speaks I slap him; his face will be one big bruise in the morning. He looks as if he is about to faint and I want to stop suddenly, but then I wonder how many times his wife has wanted to faint and he kept going despite it. Crack, crack, crack. I unseal his lips so we can hear his hurt. I'm sorry, he says, and then his eyes widen in surprise. It is his wife's voice that is emerging plaintive from his mouth.

I slap him again. Please, he begs, stop.

All it is, I say, grunting with effort, is lipstick.

When I speak, I speak in his voice. Now if it were left up to me I could kill him. But it is my mother who stops me. Who puts a hand on my shoulder and says, Enough. By now, my whole face is red with lipstick. I step back for a second and smile at him.

Then, I wave my hand and he is released. He begins to weep in his own voice, starts to try to run again and stumbles in his relief to find he has control of his limbs again.

My mother hugs me, and something in me starts to soar. All those years ago, my mother held me when Naila aunty came down and screamed at the sight of her limp son, at the sight of her husband lying in the doorway of the study—and oh, then something miraculous happened. We saw her transform into us.

Naila aunty ran right up to the study and began to kick Mansoor uncle as my mother and I watched, invisible as always, and her voice was ours when she asked her husband, Did you do this to him like you do this to me every night? She fell on him like a wild animal, she kicked his stomach and his face over and over again. And then she left him there. When Mansoor uncle came to a half hour later, he did not look at his wife or his son, he crawled on his hands and feet out the door. Previously, we had moved weekly, sometimes daily. But we stayed on at Naila aunty's that night, and then the night after and then the night after. My mother thought I needed to witness Naila aunty's life of freedom for as long as it took me to see its existence meant I was worthy of forgiveness.

When the mob arrives at the dome, they find nothing on the stage except a few drops of blood, some long strands of hair. I am away, washing my face in one of the park's ponds. Later, my mother and I walk back and sit side by side on the stage. My mother traces the dried stains of blood with her finger. It is our job to make sure they are okay, she says.

I feel older, I am finally beginning to understand what my life will be like. The stars hang low in the sky. But who will make sure I am okay?

Naila aunty was glorious that day, as powerful as us, and ready to murder her way into life. That is why I think of her often. I saw myself in her, and if I am in her, then maybe I am in every woman, and there is no use for the work we do at all.

I don't think they need us, I tell my mother. And the words are a relief. I have never said them out loud and they have been waiting in my mouth all these years. I stop myself from adding please.

My mother glances at me. You wouldn't do this if it was up to you, right?

I think of the rage I'd felt that afternoon, and all the strength that had collected in my body. But all of it is diluted in memory now.

I wouldn't, I admit.

They need us, she says. And for the first time ever I think, What she means is she needs me. The park is big. The greenery around us is like a solid weight on our bodies. This life is a gift, my mother whispers when we lie down on the stage. Her voice is soft and hypnotic and she uses her arms to make snow angels absently. Hair gets caught between her arms and the concrete. For a second I almost believe her before my mind asserts itself. Even a churail like my mother wants her life to be witnessed. She wants to be mine, she wants me to be hers. Even now Naila aunty lives under the shadow of who she was to others.

HOW TO RAISE AMERICAN CHILDREN

When the man you have been dating for three years, exactly half your time in America, asks you to marry him, do not think, Damn, he's white. Think, I love him. Think, This is the love of my life.

Travel home to tell your mother. Take a plane. Speak of nothing on the drive from the airport to the house. Once you get there, lose no time. Make yourself sit in the black chair your father had a heart attack in twenty years ago. It's starting to peel and reveal soft, yellow foam inside. Maybe the chair is actually your father's body reincarnated, come to listen. Speak firmly. Project your voice, I want to marry him. When your mother is bewildered, repeating, A white man?, over and over again, maintain your laissez-faire attitude. Say, Yes. I want to marry him. For good measure, add, I just don't want a life like yours. Pretend not to see the hurt on your mother's face. Eat a biscuit politely. You are almost thirty. Say, He'll convert, and turn a deaf ear to the hard, sarcastic way she says, Really? Finally, when she says, You were supposed to come back. Who will your children be?

stand and gesture toward the house that she has lived in quietly for years now. Spiderwebs map the corners of the living room, a cleaning lady pours water on the porch outside. Ask gently because you genuinely want to know, Do you really want them to be from here? Tell her you're tired when she says, But you're from here. Restate the facts as known by you. Say, I love him. Say, I'm flying back in two weeks. Will you come? Pretend to be happy when she says yes and then later, surprised when she does not get the visa in time. For so long, before you moved, it was just the two of you. Isn't it time for you to belong just to yourself for a while?

Tell your husband-to-be about the visa situation during a long afternoon spent in bed. When he says, We can wait, hold his cock gently in your hands and say, Do you really want to wait? Watch confusion pass across his face before his eyes clear. Try not to feel hurt when he moves your hand away and says, This isn't a movie. Do not blurt out, I want to spend my life feeling like I live in a movie, I want Starbucks for life, dollars and dollars, vacations near waterfalls, that's why I'm here! Bite your tongue as he gets out of bed to make dinner. He bakes potatoes every other day. Jokingly say to his naked back, I've never had so many potatoes in my life! Feel yourself begin to suffocate, imagine it is potatoes pulling you under, that smooth yellow mush up your nose, clogging your throat. Wave him away when he comes running at the sound of you hyperventilating. Feel relieved when he says, Okay!, after you manage to eke out, No more potatoes, between breaths.

When your mother arrives for the wedding you postponed for her, make sure she has the right expectations. This isn't that sort of wedding, no choreographed dances, no mithai, no gold. Watch her face fall farther and farther down a hole of *whose daughter is this*? Do not start to cry when she says, An American wedding, as if she is tasting the words in her mouth, even if you are always only a minor cliff away from wails, from wondering if you *do* want choreographed dances, mithai, gold, lines of relatives waiting to greet the groom. Be stoic. And then surprise yourself by giving her a hug. Hold her for longer than you expected. Say, Thank you for coming, only cry a little (one or two tears maximum) when she hugs you back and says, I love you. Wonder only for a millisecond how you came to be here, holding your mother's old bones in your arms so far from home, and why you thought that would be a good idea.

On your wedding day, watch your mother stand at the door of the new-age American restaurant you and your husband have chosen as a venue. Watch as she greets the guests, Hello, I am the mother of the bride. Do not resent the incessant mothering, the way she labels herself in relation to you without being asked. Instead smile benignly as charcuterie boards are passed around. When his friends ask, Do you eat salami? say, No, it's for you, and gesture magnanimously at the food to hide your embarrassment. Give your mother a warning glance when she overhears and comes to whisper in your ear, Do not spend your life being a caterer to this country. Clasp your now-husband's hand, kiss him full on the mouth, let the whoops of congrats swallow you whole. Now the day is a song, now the day is a prison and when it is coming to an end, let yourself be led to a corner by your mother. Hide your laughter when she says, Are you prepared for the wedding night? These white men know how to thrust from all that surfing, which can be both a blessing and a curse. Assure her your husband doesn't know how to swim, has never caught a fish, doesn't like the beach. Tell her, I'll be fine, and look away from her eyes when you say it so she does not see you wondering, Will you?

Let your new husband drive her to the airport, her in the passenger seat, you in the back. Let him wait in the car while you take her to the mouth of the departures gate. Allow yourself to feel moved when the wave of people walking past you parts. Give her a moment to take off the bangle she's always worn around her wrist. This was your grandmother's. Slip the bangle on your arm as she quietly adds, A girl is divided in two after she marries. Feel the needle always hanging above your head drop gently, cleave you slowly into halves. Watch one half leave with your mother. Let the other stay to live here, apart from her.

Watch as the shadow of you follows your mother home to an empty house. Watch your mother unpack slowly, watch her think, Tomorrow I have to call the plumber. Watch as she calls her sister—your aunt—to say, Yes, I'm back, everything went well, the boy was really nice. Realize she never says his name, it sounds foreign in her mouth. The joy and the curse of being a shadow is that you can see but you cannot interfere. Now your mother is old, stumbling over furniture, watching the windows at night, learning how to drive in the afternoons. Watch how she misses not your father exactly, so long dead that he is fading in memory now, but a companion. Wonder how a life can get smaller and wider at the same time. Do not think too much when she stops turning on the lights at night, preferring to stay glued to her phone instead, first watching dramas and then flicking through photos. Let the part of you left with her feel the full weight of the past she lives in. Think only sometimes of the father leaving in the mornings for work, the mother waiting for you in the afternoons when you arrived from school, the long sticky summer afternoons spent with cousins, an uneasy, sweltering adolescence. Wonder is it her life or your own you are watching? Only sometimes is it clear that it is your mother: your mother with her sisters, your mother with her brothers, your mother with her own parents, your mother a person you did not see until now, as defined as this, as lonely as this. Look for the straight line that led from your mother's life to your life being lived here, with her and also there with that other part of you busy becoming someone else: wife of one, yoga practitioner, killer of cockroaches, thankfully the sex is good, Mama.

And now come back to the half aloft in a country that is slowly becoming your own. The First Amendment is the right to free speech, the Second the right to bear arms. Everything here begins with the word *right*. So design the life lived here in neat orderly lines, let the life there recede away. Now the country you grew up in is dotted far away on the horizon. Who do we become when we are not someone's children? Let this question visit your home, seeping into the small sigh of a second after you've just taken the kettle off the stove and are staring into the vacuum of an endless evening, let it creep into some sunsets, rare arguments with your husband, let it mar the word *idyllic* when you begin to think of your life as such, and finally let it enter and stay in the stream of the late afternoon filled with the first cry of your newborn child—a son. Here finally is the question, in the middle of becoming an answer.

Do not be sad when your mother cannot come for the baby's birth, she is older now, Bring the child to me. Remember, we drown not in great gasping gulps but slowly, accepting that we must flow in the direction of life. This child is your child but is also not, his skin lighter than yours. He is a box waiting to be marked Other on forms in this country. Do not be surprised when the people in this other country become strangers. Call your mother and say, I do not have a measure for his childhood because I have not lived a version of it, and who will this child be? Be grateful when she does not say, I told you so. Say thank you when she tells you (daily now), It gets easier.

Allow yourself the mercy of letting it get easier. A year into motherhood, travel back with your husband to the country you grew up in—it's his first time here—and don't be surprised when you find some satisfaction in watching him flounder in the rush of the airport, at driving on the other side of the road, the way these people (my people) move to laws both invisible and collectively known. Accept the teas, the invitations to dinner, have sex in the bedroom you grew up in and meet your other half there above the bed—you were a girl and now you have returned as a woman. Let your mother spend a day explaining the history of the house to your husband, join him on the tour. Remember that yes, they decorated the house together, your mother and your father, they spent months going to nurseries in the city, bringing home plants, lining them outside the main door. The echo of your parents' life as it was lived together still hums like hope in the house. The night before you are due to go back, stand with your knees pressed against a corner of the bed, the baby asleep on the mattress, your husband standing behind you. Let your husband take you from behind, let him thrust and thrust until you have managed to obliterate the words *I don't want to go back* from every part of your body where they could find a home. The next day, break away (again) from your mother's orbit, fly back with your husband and your child. Be grateful for the rest of your life that you hugged her for as long as you did when saying goodbye.

It is a heart attack, in her sleep. You saw her three months ago. Now she is dead but how strange that you are still orbiting her. Fly back for the funeral, arrive with the house full of relatives, some you have not seen for years. Tell them you need a second alone with the house, do not mince words, do not flinch when one of her brothers stops on his way outside to tell you, Things are not important, as if this is supposed to be a balm. Do not allow them to take weight away from the things she spent her last years with. In your grief, try to remember that your life without her is still a life. But still, watch the half of you that lived with her drift across the empty rooms, your orbit of your mother changed only in that now you orbit her absence, crooning, She was alone, she was alone, she was alone.

———

Stay for a while in the country that raised you. Go to her grave daily to meet yourself there, cajole yourself to come back to you. Finally, five weeks later, fly back to your husband and child and state, You are my life, like a declaration. When your son is asleep at night, sing him lullabies in your language. Say, You are mine, to make him so and ignore the ghost of your mother always sitting in a corner of his room, laughing. Plead with her, I'm sorry, I love you, until she leaves. Descend into sleep that is not sleep at night. Travel back to the garden your mother grew behind the house. That half of you, so long separated, lives there now. Tell her, I have come to take you home. I am so sorry, I did not know how much it would hurt to live my own life, to watch her grow old from a distance, to ignore the weekly crackle of loneliness over a phone line. I can't live like this anymore, now is it time to start anew? Watch your other half pull a zucchini off the stem of a plant, gather a few tomatoes. Concede when she offers them to you. Maybe one day this house will be torn down, and you too will grow into your life as a new mother, embed your heart in your children and then help them give it back to you. For now bite into the tomatoes your mother grew. It is your heart that is ravenous. Let that old gleaming needle suture you whole as she feeds the two of you again.

ACKNOWLEDGMENTS

Thank you to my agent, Samantha Shea, whose faith in my writing has kept me writing. Thank you to Brigid Hughes, editor extraordinaire, for seeing this book clearly and helping me see it better too. Thank you to the whole team at *A Public Space*, including Anne McPeak, Janet Hansen, Francesca Richer, Kait Astrella, Aditi Bhattacharjee, Alexandra Tilden, and Lydia Mathis. Ruby Wang and Megan Cummins are no longer at *A Public Space*, but they also played a big role in shepherding these stories into the world.

Thank you to the University of East Anglia, MacDowell, Yaddo, and Hedgebrook for affording me writing time, space, and community when I needed it most.

I would not be the writer and person I am today without the friendship of Bikram Sharma. May there be another fifty years of sustained conversations in our future. And thank you to Yewande Omotoso—I remain in awe of the way you embody the titles of mother, daughter, sister, writer, and friend.

A big thank-you also to my workshop buddies who taught me so much during a few short months—Lana Lin, Chet'la Sebree, and Jackie Wang.

Thank you to my first community in the United States, and to friendships that have endured through both distance and time—to Dana Inez, Nikay Paredes, Chelsea Snow, Will Vincent, Marguerite Bennett.

For their support, Garth Risk Hallberg, Kevin Wilson, Sohini Basak, Jocelyn Nicole Johnson, and Tom Conaghan.

For unexpected and lasting friendships (and for gossiping with me)—Haider Shahbaz, Amna Chaudhry, and John Kim. And for my best friends Natalia Naveed, Fatima Rizvi, Unum Babar, Sahar Alamgir, Shahrnaz Kemal, Palki Ahmad. Your lives change my life every day.

With thanks for their support and encouragement, Abseen Anya and Hayden Blain.

Finally, this book is for my mother, Shahnaz Sohail, and my late father, Sohail Amin. Every story is about you. For my second mother, Shaheena Anjum (Green Ammi) and for my brothers, Ali Anjum, Faisal Sohail, and Taimoor Sohail.

And of course, everything is for my son, Zemar Sohail-Teffera, and for Teff. I am lucky to have and to love you.